Post-Apocalyptic Apocalyptic Policing

With Frida

KAHLO
Koj Books

CONTENTS

There are things I've done I can't erase
I want to look in the mirror see another face
I said, "never", but I'm doing it again
I wanna walk away, start over again
Walk Away, Tom Waits and Kathleen Brennan

***

There was nothing he could do about the crimes that were so big you couldn't even see them.
You *lived* in them.
Jingo, Terry Pratchett

One

"When do you suppose people started having sexual fantasies?" asked Phil, taking a seat beside me. "I'm talking about human evolution. I don't think monkeys have the imagination for it. Maybe a homo erectus?"

"Been spending time at the library, Phil?" I asked, looking across the street at the third floor of our book repository. Our reformed police department rated nowhere near as important to our reconstituted city of Rochester as the IT and communications teams who worked over there.

"I've done a little reading," said Phil, "but you have to wonder what sort of brainpower is needed to imagine and fantasize."

"To say nothing of a person's circumstances. I doubt any prehistoric human spent time imagining sex without having it. What made you think of this?"

"Thinking about who else might be able to think more than we expect."

"Phil, don't go there."

I spent the next few weeks on guard duty because Sarge heard I hated spending time by the fences. I had no idea this would be my last conversation with Phil before he moved out of the barracks and spent all his time on the bridge overlooking the zombie pens.

***

I heard the car before I could see it. In recent months, few unexpected vehicles approached the city fences and those that did sounded near complete breakdown. This hatchback limped, quivered, and headed directly at me.

Standing on the inside of the Rochester barrier, I dealt with the occasional curious zombie, but the signs scattered for miles around directed refugees to our actual gate. The fencing near me offered no opening. My skillset did not include evaluating the few people who found their way to the flower city. Most people preferred refuge further east or north.

I did not believe the stories about Canada being a haven. In the other direction, New Jersey held my childhood home, but I felt safest inside Rochester.

I waved vigorously at the driver and any passengers. About twenty feet out, they turned sidewise which gave me hope they would head for the gate. The driver tried to read my lips.

"Go to the gate! It's a half mile straight along. Careful of the ditch over there!" I conveyed too much information.

In the distance, I saw the reason I hated the outside world. Rumors suggested great herds of the undead roamed in the uninhabited expanse between reclaimed pockets of civilization. We only saw groups in the dozens, but those disturbed me enough.

Signaling more furiously, I pulled muscles until the car doors opened. My arms drooped to my sides when the driver cut the car engine.

Two adults and two children stepped into the evening sun, casting long shadows reaching to my feet. I pointed and yelled, "Zombies!"

"Let us in!"

"Help us!"

"The car is out of gas!"

"Where's the goddamn gate?"

I looked to the top of the fence, rising twenty feet over my head. "The nearest gate is a half mile that way! Didn't you see the signs?"

The adults considered the distances involved and performed rapid calculations. I scanned my surroundings for any bright ideas. Our superiors made sure we had no wire cutters. The authorities punished offenders by expulsion for aiding breachers. I made calculations of my own.

I ran and grabbed my pack based on my best guess where this headed.

When I returned, I watched the adults help the children onto the fence. I passed them a sweatshirt and a jacket to wrap around their hands to protect against the barbs.

By the time the children climbed five feet, the zombies had closed half the distance. The adults exchanged a look and a nod. They turned to me. The woman's expression summarized so much loss she dared me to call this a surrender.

"What's your name?" she demanded.

"Alonzo Crash!" I yelled because adrenalin is a significant amplifier.

"No! Your real name?" She did not wait for an answer. "I'm Sheila Jacobs. He's Nate Wallace. The boy is Curtis and... and..." Her voice petered out. "I can't remember!"

I mouthed my real pre-apocalypse name, but she gave no sign of understanding. No one had spoken those words since we emerged into this new world. Old names lingered everywhere for places and things, but the people of Rochester had rechristened themselves *en masse* because we could not look at each other after what we had done to survive. This boiled the wisdom of our trials down to a single act.

I did the most helpful thing allowed and lit incense torches. The current batch consisted of citronella candles looted from a Home Depot. I jabbed them into the ground and hoped for the best. They might hide whatever scent lured the undead.

The adults ran back to their car and retrieved a jumble of weapons which they laid out on the hood. They had a revolver and two shotguns which they used to reduce the horde. They took out about a quarter of the approaching pack before they switched to swords.

The man's sword broke like a mail-order replica. He did not scream as the zombies enveloped him. Instead, he wrapped as many as possible in his arms until his strength ebbed. The woman slashed and backed in my direction. She punctuated her movements with screams at the children to hurry.

The young ones did their best, but the horror show entranced them. I added my encouragement to the woman's. Nothing prodded them and I knew how this would end.

A pile up presented the main danger to any barrier. The undead would move against the obstacle. Others would climb onto their backs. The next one surmounts them both. If you have enough zombies, then you have a slope to the top of your barrier.

Transfixed well behind the citronella stakes, I watched the undead devour the woman. I continued to yell at the children, but the girl would not move. The boy tugged on her until the first zombie grabbed her foot.

Becoming spectators, the boy and I watched as the undead rose toward him. I could not see his face. So many go mute when faced with this ultimate vision. The undead smell and crackle and evacuate disgusting sounds. But seeing those dented, corroded, masticating faces defies response. We do not go limp, and we do not stop fighting, but recognition of the inevitable arrives. Otherwise, no one could stand there and watch the boy die, and I owed it to him.

I had never seen anyone from the car before they pulled up to the fence, but my version of coming to terms with this zombie-scape of a world meant I treated every sacrifice with respect and dignity, no matter how stupid, asinine, brave, or glorious.

It also supplied the best description of what life had become: stupid, asinine, brave, and glorious.

***

The bell on the old ice cream truck always attracted the zombies. Simmons enjoyed playing the song because he clung to his sick sense of humor. The truck no longer carried ice cream. Instead, Simmons delivered lunches along the fence lines.

I saw the wave of zombies breaking on the fences as Simmons approached, performing as their Siren.

I am sick and tired of zombies. I hate them. My shift on the fences had almost ended. This duty turn had been peaceful compared to most. A thousand yards up the line, I watched the Rock go to the truck and retrieve his rations. The lunch ladies usually put in a cookie for those of us stationed on the edge of the city.

I stood with my back to the fence and waited for Simmons to park and turn off the engine. He left the tune going for an extra few seconds because I wanted it to stop. Hitting the fences, the undead sounded like raw meat dropping onto a tin roof. Later, I would have to puncture the brainpans of the trapped, undying undead and pry them backwards off the wire barbs.

Simmons passed me my meal without moving from the driver's seat. "Rochester thanks you for your service."

"Why do you have to antagonize them?" I asked. I peered inside my meal to see how I would feel about it later. I saw a cookie, which encouraged me.

"Why wouldn't I antagonize them?" Simmons pointed over my head. "They're the reason I'm driving this stupid thing and have this terrible job. I'd like to do more than antagonize them."

"But you don't have to stick around after they're all riled up."

Simmons started the engine, "It's all part of the service I offer." He stopped his hand before it reached the music switch. "For you, this one time. Sarge said he'd be paying you a visit later." He drove off and waited almost fifty yards before restarting his terrible song.

I steeled myself before turning around and facing the fences. We had strung chain-link and barbed wire between posts buried deep in cement. Other places around the border of the city, we had stopped the undead with rock or other available objects.

I walked to my table forty feet back from the barrier.

After a while, I heard a bicycle arrive followed by the sound of familiar footsteps. Sarge sat down beside me. He went everywhere riding his 18-speeder, which explained his enormous calves. As he sat, his groan signified his age.

After a snort, he said, "Am I looking at a Honda Civic?" He pointed at the car beyond the offal pile on the other side of the fence.

"Yes, I think so," I agreed. "A family drove up."

"Didn't they see the signs? They should have followed the arrows." Sarge pushed himself upright and walked toward the barrier. "The fence looks undamaged, which is something at least. Still, the Mayor will want to send somebody out to confirm everything is all right."

I nodded because we had a hierarchy, and you nod when your superior makes a pronouncement. Sarge turned his back to me to pay respects to the recently reconsecrated ground.

Sarge sagged a little as he turned back, but he pulled up tall when he caught me noticing. He sat down again, suppressing the accompanying exhalation. "I wanted to talk something over with you, so I came out here."

When he did not continue, I said, "Simmons told me to expect you."

"He's all right, but he's misplaced one of his knitting needles and he's coming undone." The next pause ended sooner. "I'm thinking we need a detective willing to leave headquarters."

"I noticed Sherlock around the place a lot more."

"He mostly stays on the roof," said Sarge. "He doesn't bother anyone, so I'm giving him time. Meanwhile, I'd like you to do some investigating."

I motioned outside the fence. "Do we really need a detective? Explanations are obvious these days."

Sarge turned away so I barely heard him. "We still have the occasional enigma. You'll do better than most."

I made a joke, "Is there a pay raise?"

"In your dreams," said Sarge as he rose again. "I even have a case for you."

I tamped down my interest, "Yeah?"

"There's a woman with a cat down in the reclaimed ward. Go take the kitty away from the nice lady. Make this city proud."

Two

I found myself on my bike heading to the South Wedge the next morning. The spring air blew off the sun-lit lake, which prevented me smelling the retention pens until I crossed over them. If you lived in the city, you could tolerate the stench to some extent.

Wearing a rebreather, Phil stood on the bridge over what used to be I-490. I don't know how he did it every day, but the man hadn't missed a shift in two years, though everyone knew why. Less inclined toward punctuality and reliability, I would have missed more than a few shifts. The word at the barracks had him taking all the shifts for the last few weeks. We all break in different ways in our own time.

After the end of the world, the phrase "Crazy Cat Lady" took on a more sinister meaning. Infestations became far more urgent. The issue used to be smell and clutter, not rumors about returning pets. The Mayor worried about widespread panic.

I pulled my kerchief over my face as I dismounted and walked the bike down the middle of the road. Most days I avoided looking over the edge of the bridge.

Gate guards had mostly stopped putting on full gear, but stagnant days came along when the smell proved too much for anyone to bear.

"Hey, how are they today?" I asked.

"Same old, same old, the way I like it." Through the face mask, Phil's voice sounded dim and round as if from a cave. His eyes shared a tunnel vision appearance with many of us.

"Any familiar faces?"

Soon as I spoke, I regretted it. Phil waved me over. I ambled toward him after putting the bike against a pile of rubble. I focused on the sky for a second before lowering my gaze.

Interstate 490 ran through the center of Rochester. Soon as it hit downtown, it shot a spur around the northern edge before joining back up with the main line at the end of the city. This once formed a large loop around downtown. Choosing the southern arc because the highway planners had dug it deep into the ground, survivors walled off and covered with fencing a large section of the loop.

Looking over the edge, a roof of chicken wire stretched into the distance. Beneath it, the zombies meandered. I tried to maintain my focus on the crosshatch no more than a feet beneath us, so I wouldn't have to look at the walking cadavers. Survivors chose to keep these meandering dead, family or worth saving for another reason. I knew more about the latter since I had spent the first year of the plague hiding in a science lab at the University of Rochester. We experimented on the reanimated when not fighting for survival. No one fit the bill for me to keep.

Phil nudged me. He'd been talking while I tried to maintain my equilibrium.

"There's my Becky," said Phil.

I let my eyes focus where he pointed. Becky didn't look as bad as others did.

"It rained overnight. They always look a little better after the rain, at least the ones who stay out of the mud." Phil said.

"I have to head down to the Wedge. Can you let me out?"

Phil frowned.

About a year previous, we had extended the city protection to encompass the Wedge neighborhood, a dangling area south of the freeway. Most folks will not set foot outside the original downtown fences. Those barriers represented the difference between life and death for all of them. A couple hundred people moved to the reclaimed land, barely enough to justify the effort, but the city needed somewhere for new arrivals.

"You be careful out there," said Phil.

"I will do my best." I turned back to him. "I'll see you on my way back over."

"I'll be counting the minutes." The facemask disguised the degree of Phil's sarcasm.

The air hung heavy with zombie stink on the south side of the retention pens, so I kept my nose covered as I rode. The university lay on the far side of the reclaimed Wedge. As my first pass since entering the fortified city, I didn't recognize the area from my last desperate run to safety.

Now it reminded me of tornado damage— the way a funnel cloud will dip and spin, randomly picking out houses here and there— a map of lives randomly lost or spared. I passed houses in undamaged condition. The difference here was people didn't rebuild. Demand had been low, so trailblazers could choose a home which had withstood the zombie ravages. They might be loners or those with a past to hide. Or weird cat ladies...

A family sat on their front porch looking like the last few years had never happened, except now a family became an entirely self-defined unit. People found each other during the worst times and did not let go after whatever they had seen together. Petty differences proved manageable. When the violence settled down and people had quiet time to look at one other, they chose to stay with those who had seen them at their worst.

I took a right on Alexander Street. I sought a house on the left about halfway down inhabited by a woman named Irene. According to the complaint, Irene worried someone enough to haul themselves into the station to report her cat, unlikely to be a false alarm.

I found the house. After leaning the bike against a car in the driveway, I climbed the porch carefully. The steps creaked loudly, forewarning any occupants. Between people's penchant for booby traps and poor maintenance skills, I worried more about being hurt on those few steps than confronting Irene. I knocked and stepped back.

"Who's there?" came her voice.

"Police officer, ma'am."

"Really?"

"Yes, ma'am."

The door opened slowly. She tilted her head and considered me. "Look at you." About my age, Irene had a comparable way of scanning her surroundings. All survivors looked frayed at the edges. "Is this you being neighborly?"

"Sort of, ma'am. May I come in?"

"How do I know you're really a cop?"

Police uniforms are not so uniform anymore. Most of us go in for a dark blue shirt and a pair of jeans. I pulled out a badge and showed it to her. "My name is Alonzo Crash."

"Your badge doesn't mean a thing and you know it." She stared hard enough to make me blink. "Ah, hell, come on in. At least, you're not one of them."

I heard the cause of my visit. First the whiskers and then a full cat face peered around a doorway.

"Can I offer you anything? Water? Tea?" asked Irene.

Hospitality had become uncommon even if people let you past the door. "Tea sounds nice if it's not too much trouble." I followed her to the kitchen, aware of the cat behind me.

Whether squatters or not, most folks rearranged their living quarters. Irene's kitchen had been a family room once upon a time. She had built a small brick oven in the corner. A cot leaned against the wall. A nester, she did not use more of the house. After pouring water from a plastic jug into a teakettle, she placed it on the brick oven. "It'll be a few minutes."

I pulled out a notepad. The cat wandered into the room and jumped onto the cot. It clawed a little and then settled in. I confirmed her full name: Irene Dickinson; and she lived alone.

The kettle whistle interrupted us. With tea in our hands, we sat in her only two chairs.

Irene sighed. "You don't remember me, do you?"

I tried. She wore overalls which didn't fit and a long-sleeved shirt. Anyone could be somebody or nobody. She wanted me to think back on the times I had submerged inside myself.

"I attended U. of R.," said Irene. "You hid in a lab in the basement. No one made it in the labs upstairs... almost no one. Tim and I did."

"I'm sorry, but I try not to carry history."

"Professor Timothy Shankar. He taught microbiology," Irene clarified.

One name provided all it took to surface the past. "I had him. Is he still around?"

"He left one night. I made it to another classroom and hid. A couple people had a bunker with scavenged food from the cafeteria stores. I thought I could be safe with them." She stared at the floor. "I might have seen Shankar since, changed into one of them."

Looking at her through the tea steam, I couldn't perceive her as anyone I recognized.

She looked at me, "No one ever wants to talk about college or anything about before..." She spoke the truth.

I said, "You're probably wondering why I'm here."

"Not so much." A twinkle in her eye reminded me of life in the old days, though her gleam left me longing for a world forever out of reach. "Friendly company is rare in the South Wedge. I wanted my pick of the houses, so I moved back before others. I arrived with all the early adoption misanthropes. I suppose I'm one, too."

I could not decide which way to go on her misanthropy. "So, you didn't grow up in Rochester?"

"I said I wanted my pick of the houses, but I didn't say why. I grew up in this house. My parents both taught at the University. They had class on campus the day those things overran it. We all were over there, including you."

I nodded. "March 9."

She sipped her tea and looked at the cat. "I lied earlier."

"What about?"

"I want to know why you're here."

I sighed. The tea tasted good, but I would not have the opportunity to finish it.

"It's about the cat. City ordinances expressly prohibit pets within the city walls. You don't have to put it down. The city has set up a shelter where—"

"Shut up. Shut up. Shut up!" She tossed her teacup across the room. The shatter of it gave her pause. "You don't know me. You don't know what I might do. You come here and you want to take away my only friend? Who put you up to this?"

On my feet, I said, "Nobody put me up to this, Irene. It's the law."

"Don't you dare call me Irene! You aren't allowed!"

"All right, Ms. Dickinson, let's calm down. We can talk about this."

She worked her mouth a little, but no words came out. Then she burst into tears and rose to her feet, knocking over my teacup.

I tried to tell her it would be all right. She could always visit her cat. I turned my attention to the feline, shiny black fur with golden eyes. Calmly, it stared back at me.

"Does the cat have a name?"

Irene sniffled, "Onyx."

I cooed at the cat and took one slow step. Those eyes watched and the paws held still. I scooped it off the cot and it nestled into my arms. "Good kitty."

Irene leapt on my back and pulled my hair. The cat flew out of my arms. I spun around, wrenched Irene's fingers back, and flailed. As her grip loosened, Irene crashed into a wall. She crumpled to the floor and wept. I cursed and ran after the cat. In the dining room, I found an open window. Onyx perched in a tree in the front yard. By the time I reached her, Onyx had long gone. I yelled at the sky for a while and kicked the dirt.

Unwilling to admit failure back at the station, I sat down on Irene's porch steps. Our force existed to serve the interests of the Mayor with outliers like me serving the public interest.

I scanned up and down the street. A quiet day and I doubted a cat would make enough noise for me to hear. I squinted, but nothing crept into view.

"No luck, super cop?" Irene sat down beside me. She had smeared her face where she had wiped away tears.

I shrugged. Most people twisted their emotions in small circles. "The world is a big place." In the last few years, I had learned to operate on a different scale because of all the crazy. Most people lived their lives on the edge of the precipice, and they deserved leeway.

"Why does it feel like it's been shrinking these past few years?" She forced a smile. "Onyx won't come back after all the kerfuffle."

"If you've been feeding her and she's been sleeping here, then...," I said.

"What's the big deal?" Irene said.

"She could be a carrier." Like everyone, I heard the stories about the start of the plague. Rumors circulated it had crossed over from other species. Some people spent their spare time hunting feral pets to near extinction.

"You know that isn't how it works. You need to die or be bitten by another zombie," Irene said.

"Not everybody agrees with you. Those people who worry are your neighbors," I said. "The last thing you need is for them to worry about you. The police force is nothing like it used to be. Nobody is going to protect you if anybody has a bad idea in their head."

"Retaliation," said Irene.

"What?"

"It's all we're any good for anymore. We don't stop things beforehand. We can only retaliate after the fact," said Irene.

"I think I'm trying to head off a problem right now," I said.

"The cat ran away; I hate to tell you."

In silence for a time, we considered the bigger message this entailed.

"Tell me something," I asked, "how'd you earn a place to yourself?"

"I moved in. Give a girl a little time to register."

"You'll probably end up with housemates," I said.

"Don't remind me."

The trees had bloomed. Magnolia scent drifted on the wind.

"Your car looks better than most."

"A giant paperweight without gasoline." Irene stood up and stretched. "I know the government is back and such. I could make a telephone call if I found a way to charge a cell phone. But I don't expect to drive a car ever again." She gave me a sad look. "You can wait here all you like, but I'm not so comfortable with open spaces anymore. I'm going inside."

I peered in both directions and saw nothing like a black cat. "What will you do if it dies?"

"Bury it, I imagine. I know what people think, but I've never heard of a cat coming back."

"Plenty of people say they do."

"Lots of things don't," said Irene. "If insects did, then we'd have been done a long time ago; same with rats and raccoons."

"Cows do."

"I know." She climbed the stairs. "Of course, we eat cows." She went inside.

"People eat bugs," I said to no one in particular.

THREE

T he Public Safety Building never stopped being police headquarters. The first floor lost the street-side exterior wall during
the tough times, but the remaining officers did their best to repair it.
Like humanity's other recent accomplishments, the fix looked like a
giant scar on aged skin. The building appeared mostly empty.

None of the force specialties existed anymore, meaning traffic enforcement ceased as a thing. Despite my promotion, the distinction
between detective and street cop did not exist for practical purposes.
Society could not be less interested in internet crime or illegal arms.
If you could log onto the internet, then more power to you. Everyone
had a gun or needed one. The laws might be in the books (wherever
those books might be), but we saved the enforcement for a brighter
day. The entire force consisted of young people with a smattering of
police survivors around to keep the rest of us in line. The Mayor made
the rules, and we enforced them.

At the front desk, Hazel and Jared dealt with the public. Hazel
faced a guy in a business suit complaining about white-collar crime.

Reassured anyone worried about making money again, I could see Hazel had no idea how to proceed. I caught Jared's attention and asked him about the cat report from the South Wedge.

"A kid with long hair. He said his Mom sent him. I passed it along to Sarge."

"Thanks, Jared. I'll talk to the man."

I found Sarge on the second floor. One of those old cops frowned at me from across the room. "I don't see any cat," he bellowed. "I hope it's because it's a bogus report."

"No, Sarge, the cat exists, but he escaped…"

He shook his head and sauntered to his office. The job allowed the time for him to find someone less useless than me. The applicant pool existed, but our on-the-job training filtered out most would-be police. Nobody knew how to train us anyway, assuming anyone could define our current responsibilities.

Sarge popped back out. "All right, you lay-a-bouts, spread the word. Tomorrow is a big day. We're sending folks outside the fence on the west side to do clean up. The mayor wants the highway to look acceptable because we have freight coming in from Jersey. They'll want to continue to Buffalo so we need to make sure the convoy has no trouble in our territory. If you prefer, you can do crowd control for the unloading and distribution. I have two clipboards here. If you want to keep your godforsaken job, then your name is going to be on one of them by the end of the day."

He slammed the boards down on a desk and stalked back into his office. No one rushed to volunteer for either assignment. A couple of the cowboys moseyed over first and made sure they went outside to guard and shoot.

I had not set foot beyond the fences since I left the university basement. Before my visit with Irene, I had not returned to the South Wedge. My name went on crowd control.

Returning to my desk, I spent time on paperwork. The resurrection of the government meant the rebirth of bureaucracy. I wrote down my observations during my travels so anyone with a terminal could enter the information into the computer system.

Officers had occasional electricity, but the city's IT department had power all the time. They kept us in touch with the rest of the world. A bunch of IT people barricaded in the old building of the central library became our lifeline. Two floors down, somebody found the library servers and the network and knew what to do. They may have helped save civilization, but they are a bunch of know-it-alls so who wants to tell them?

Once the city government returned, the computer wizards occupied as much of the library as they wanted. Volunteer librarians wandered around keeping the books in place and running the checkout parts of the operation, but City IT filled the remaining cubbyholes.

After I finished the report and left it in the appropriate pile, I rubbed my wrists. Many of us found using pens and pencils again rough going. In the old days of computer word processors on every desk, no teacher ever told me my penmanship would mean the difference between a police job and maintaining boundary fences.

I knew quite a few people could not manage work anymore, but the alternative proved worse. You lived in one of the shelters and you had nothing to do. We all said we wouldn't judge them, but it became tougher every day we moved closer to normal.

When the police HQ returned, they placed the mess hall one floor upstairs. They kept the food on the floor above. The pain of hauling the bulk supplies high made sense to our siege mentality. The cafeteria cooks conjured stuff which looked like beans and whipped potatoes. It tasted all right and you learned quickly not to complain-- a benefit of the job and calories mattered.

Ethel filled out the server uniform fully and smiled when she saw me. She wanted to fatten me up and kept dumping food on my plate until I thought to withdraw my tray. Ethel lost her husband before the zombies. She hadn't heard from either of her daughters since those days. At the onset, one lived in Chicago and another in Europe, traveling with her family. Ethel used to be a partner in a law firm in the city. I learned all about her during my first week on the job. By the second week, we smiled at one another like lifelong friends.

I sat by a window alone. Over from the library, techies devoured our food, but they held their own conversation. After swallowing enough chow, I left work and headed home, around the corner.

Almost two years ago, I moved into the city garage, back then an echoing cavern next to the station. Proximity and security held more importance than two rooms and a private bath. Comfort prompted feelings of guilt. Since then, we subterranean dwellers had subdivided the space and torn apart the cars. We had even cleaned up a little. I had about eight parking spaces with a van and flatbed truck. In the winter, I slept in the van, and, in the summer, I slept in the back of the flatbed.

We kept the garage openings boarded up. All of us took turns on guard duty. After two years, we had enough people, so it only meant a couple of hours a night once a week. People said we had such a central location in the city we could stop with the rotation, but I needed the reassurance in order to sleep. I doubted I'd ever be ready.

The darkness had to be the worst thing about the garage. We ran lights on scavenged car batteries, but those became hard to find. Sarge had a generator which didn't do anything for the rest of us. I missed central heating. We reconfigured the layout in the deepest part of winter so we could have fires for warmth. Nobody complained about the cold months because the zombies hadn't adapted to snow and ice. If they figured out skates or snowshoes, we would be in trouble.

The techies broadcasted on two channels over the radio in the evening. One played music and the other carried children's stories. Both stations reverberated around the garage as people ran down their power sources trying to obtain a fix on the past.

Spring only occasionally suggested warm breezes, so my bedroll remained in my van. I cracked the window for air. I had to perch on the edge of the van door to read anything. My eyes tired after a few pages of an old Sports Illustrated. I missed baseball.

Nighttime in the garage never passed easily. Simmons had nightmares. We all did, but his occurred every night. The Rock snored like nobody's business. Whoever held down guard duty took the responsibility to roll him over, but most refused ever since he broke Conover's nose.

I rarely dreamt, but when I did, the images mocked my sleep. As it turned out, I spent a tough night.

I found myself talking to Irene. With the black cat in her lap, purring as she stroked it, she talked about us being old friends. She stood and took my hand. She led me out of the room and into the laboratory where I had first hidden at the university. Then she turned into a zombie. I ran away from her through the door and into the hall, a bad idea in real life and equally bad in dreamland.

The zombies waited, and I tried to run through them, but they grabbed me and wouldn't let go. They merely held me without chewing. I waited for the first awful bite, only tentative licks. The tension went on forever. Then I felt teeth sink into my calf.

I woke to Conover's pounding on the van wall. "You okay in there?" His words still sounded warped from the broken nose.

"Yea, I'm fine." I rolled over and listened to his steps recede. I counted days and realized it'd been six nights since my last nightmare. They had definitely improved.

***

Where would the country be without New Jersey? Big cities had to be the worst during the zombie crisis. The outbreak wiped away New York City and Boston, and devastated Pittsburgh. Cleveland came through all right if Rochester served as your baseline. We had no reliable information about anywhere further west. The worst hit population centers were places where people lived and worked. If you had no reason to leave your downtown home and hunkered down, then you ended up zombie chow.

Nobody with a choice lived in downtown Cleveland before the apocalypse. A handful of people lived in downtown Rochester, until the Mayor took the city back. Something similar occurred in Buffalo. I don't know what happened in Syracuse, but they popped back on the grid about the same time as us.

New Jersey came back quickly, and the national government migrated there. At least, we stopped hearing from Washington, D.C., and we all assumed they went the way of Boston. On the plus side, New Jersey made stuff which they exchanged for raw materials. They sent out convoys. They might have opened a port on the ocean.

***

Early the next day, I picked up my riot gear, tossed it in a wheelbarrow, and headed to the public market. I didn't bother suiting up. Problems arose less often as folks received food regularly and stopped feeling desperate.

Nevertheless, I liked having the gear handy until I knew the delivery would not inspire a riot. The methodology applied by our burgeoning bureaucracy spread out the population and aimed at making them easier to oversee. My own theory held bureaucracy served as the opium of the people.

A small crowd had lined up overnight. They might have been queueing for tickets for a blockbuster movie in the old days instead of rice now. We had lost significant population, but twelve thousand people still meant long lines; maybe the overnighters had the brains.

The bureaucrats planned the distribution well. As assigned, I reported to the tables for people whose last name began with the letters J, K, or L. The mousy civil servant staffing the paperwork looked grateful. I gave him a smile and slid my gym bag of gear under the table alongside his feet. We exchanged introductions. He went by Frank Jones. Everybody had a new name and a rare few fit better than others.

I heard the turnstiles open, and the populace filed in. Quickly, Frank handed me my sheet detailing my distribution. He must have grabbed it from the C pile on another table. I glanced through my list of rations; vegetables might have come in. I would have to head over to the convention center later and load the goods into my wheelbarrow.

A slight breeze felt good. Frank held his piles of paper down with stones. I couldn't make heads or tails of how he had things organized and the line moved slower than it ought. Even so, the people in the queue remained remarkably patient with friendly chatting.

The day beamed beautiful, a pleasure out among the living. People nodded greetings at me. One or two asked how I did and then ignored my answer. Sarge once said it would take another generation before we won them back because the government failed them so spectacularly.

The authorities had revealed their feet of clay. Too many people lost too much.

An angry young woman drew me back to the queue. "There's no thyme on this list. Where's my goddamn thyme?" She had the wiry look so common among all the survivors though we had seen bellies return.

I reached out to her. "There's no reason to give Mr. Jones a hard time."

"Don't you dare touch me unless you want to lose a finger" she hissed. She backed up a step and estimated me. "I suppose you're Mr. Smith?"

"Hardly— I'm Officer Crash."

She took a minute to think about the name. Her stance changed while her face betrayed nothing, "Seriously? You think up your name all by yourself?"

I ground my teeth and managed, "Not all by myself."

The line proceeded and she let out another oath.

"You'll survive without thyme this week," I offered. Glancing at her sheet, I tried to make conversation, "You live with your father?"

She gave me a look which tried to slice me into tiny pieces.

"Have a nice day!" I offered as she shuffled forward.

I watched the next people in line. In turn, each one presented their right hand to Jones, and he slathered it with green paint. Last time, he used red paint on the left hand. Only after he painted their hand did Jones look for their ration sheet. Once he found it, they signed his ledger, but he had to find them in the ledger beforehand. Overall, I wondered if we hadn't managed to bring a little piece of hell back to earth.

People made the best of it. I didn't hear any more grumbling, perhaps due to the spring air. In bad weather, the bureaucrats set up indoors. We used the Rochester Convention Center as the food distribution destination. Everybody in line at the public market had family waiting over there. It defied the logic of ease, but people accepted inconvenience. They knew about the worst. It beat sitting at home.

We reached the end of our line after five or six hours. Jones gave me a weak smile and said we had finished. I asked for the list of no shows. Someone would need to track down all six in the next day.

I tossed my gear back into the wheelbarrow and headed to the convention center. I took my time because the line would still be huge. Makeshift families filed past me with every member hauling their share. I saw so many small children carrying a can of something or other and glowing with pride. I found myself watching them, trying to see the future through their eyes, even if the future simply meant a special dinner.

Not worrying about marriage had been one of the Mayor's bolder decisions. Even so, he made the family the focus of our new social order. Any group of three or more people could register as a family. They qualified for rations together. They took responsibility for one another. At least one member had to be underage or a person otherwise needing care. This solved two big problems quickly: we had so many orphans, elderly, and differently abled. Plus, we needed to monitor everyone within the fences in case someone died. One zombie could lead to a horrific outbreak.

Fortunately, citizens found each other; not like they would have once upon a time, but it worked for Rochester. If you wanted an exception to the licensed family unit, then apply for government work. For example, cops could join a family, or we could live in the barracks. It left only random solitary souls, mostly outcasts from a group who found them too difficult to take. We hauled them into our makeshift prison where social workers tried to play matchmaker among the inmates. Others ended up in one of the maintenance staff barracks instead.

Irene had made her own solution by waiting until the city reclaimed the South Wedge before emerging from her hidey hole at the university. She would have to register soon. I needed to ensure she did.

***

The convention center survived better than most buildings. The parking garage across the street had been the scene of serious automotive carnage. Wrecks clogged the ramps, but brave souls had removed the corpses. As opposed to the garage where I lived, no one entered such a horrible place anymore. Debris blocked off the pedestrian bridges attached to the convention center. The survivors who had holed up in the Center's huge auditoriums had obstructed those.

Inside the RCC, I stayed near the outer walls and wended my way to adequate breathing room. The smell of all the unwashed humanity hung in the air like a stockyard. People had not prepared for a world without modern cosmetics and soaps. A whole segment of the community worked in sanitation and hygiene. They struggled through the chemistry, working from first principles. Still, it smelled better than the undead retention pens.

People found themselves doing hard labor after spending countless years as desk jockeys or anything else easier than their new occupations. The government rotated people through different jobs. Folks seemed happy spending their days on mind-numbing drudgery. Others did it for the distraction, some for the penance.

Against a wall guarding my wheelbarrow, I heard the voice. I turned into his embrace,

"Little brother!"

"Big brother!" I shouted.

He held me at arm's length and gave me a hard look. "You look good."

"You look like you've been on the road for a week, B," I said. When we first reunited, we bumped up against the challenge of calling one another by our new names. We settled on initials and hoped neither of us would slip.

"Looks don't deceive," said my brother.

"The trip went well?" I asked.

"Not so bad," said B. "We had a little trouble around Binghamton, but nothing we couldn't manage. One of the trucks went flat. A herd of dead ones scented us. We broke out the machine guns. Cutting them in half isn't as effective as putting one in their brain pan, but we made it through."

Somewhere during his telling, my brother realized he had an audience. While we stood in the convention center, privacy did not exist.

"And it's how we roll on the big convoy." He chucked a boy under the chin. Then he whispered to me, "Want to step outside for air?"

B grabbed my gear bag without waiting for an answer and plowed a path to the great outdoors. We gasped semi-fresh air with relief. He led us to a bench half a block away. "I hope I'm not taking you away from anything?"

"My supply collecting," I answered.

"I'm sorry," said B. "If you want anything then come around to the trucks later. We'll park by the baseball field for the night."

"I'll be fine. Rice and beans will keep."

"There's body wash this time," said B. "Somebody has production going near Hoboken and we filled one of the trucks. It's scented though I don't really recognize the smell."

"I'll have it. It'll be a big hit in the barracks." I paused, always afraid of my next words. "How're Mom and Dad?"

"Dad's not looking too good these days. You might want to think about visiting. They haven't seen you since all this started."

We sat silently as he waited for me to respond.

"Yea, I don't think so. I'll give you a letter."

He never understood my inability to leave the safety of the fences. He'd arrived from a two-day journey in the great expanse. My answer did not surprise anyone by then. He sighed heavily, but he had done his filial duty.

"Go gather your stuff before everything's gone. If you want, come by later. I'll stay by the trucks tonight; but we can always visit, if you don't have other plans, I mean." He looked at me hopefully, trawling for good news to pass along to our parents.

"I think I can swing by if nothing comes up at the station," I said.

I left him on the bench. He looked happy sitting on something stationary. Not for the first time, I thanked God for him. Somehow, he had moved our parents out of Manhattan. He claimed heading to Jersey and not Long Island happened by pure dumb luck. Long Island remained off the grid. Besides the serendipity, he managed to keep two senior citizens alive through the bad years. He still lived with them when not on the road.

Four

After I hauled my supplies to the barracks, I took the rest of the day off. Eventually, the cafeteria ladies would be around to collect the bags of bulk ingredients. For whatever reason, cops in Rochester tended not to see much action on distribution days. You'd think folks might take from one another, but people mostly behaved for a day or two, basking in the glow of plenty. These days were our slice of paradise when only good people remained, but I knew otherwise.

After supper, I decided to take a walk before I headed over to Frontier Field, where the convoy camped. I strolled down Main Street until I reached the new bakery on the corner of Stone. Normally they'd have closed earlier, but the fresh ingredients from the caravan exhilarated everyone. They did a brisk business. I found comfort in fresh bread. I bought a loaf and a half dozen croissants.

I headed off Main, toward MLK Park. We had a tiny band of insistent unhoused, but you could count them on two hands. I imagined folks who survived destitute back in the day became the first victims.

Therefore, the current crop must be new. They had to adapt to a completely different set of ground rules. We classified the park as a barracks, and the residents had to check-in with a patrol officer every day.

Once, Sarge told me the park had seen two epic battles between the living and the dead. Originally designed for outdoor concerts, its tiers and scaffolding led more than one group of survivors to think of it as the perfect place for a dramatic stand. The first time, the conflict ended in a thrilling rescue. The second battle ended in Sarge sitting on a metal perch for three days before he found an opportunity to escape. He had never gone near a ladder since I had met him.

I sat on one of the ledges and waited. The setting sun cut sharp shadows, raising my heart rate. When I heard incoherent mumbling, I didn't overreact. My response had been different the previous summer when I first met "Tragedy." No one knew his real name, so Rochester had dubbed him. He came over and sat beside me. He smelled ripe-- only body odor. He wore a brown overcoat on top of blue jeans. Someone had given him a Red Wings sweatshirt. The boots looked the same as the last time I had seen him.

"How are you?" I asked.

He looked at me hard with his gray eyes. Long salt and pepper hair hid his ears. "It's a tragedy."

"I know." I shuffled in my bakery bag. "I brought you this. You're going to need to eat it all yourself, okay? You can't give any of it to the birds. People are a little scared when they see all those wild things in one place. They might behave better if we knew how this plague started, but we don't."

"It's a tragedy." He took the bread and waved it at me, "A real tragedy."

"It sure is, my friend."

We sat and watched the rest of the sunset. Then, Tragedy wandered off, leaving me to myself.

I headed to Frontier Field. The convoy trucks filled the old Kodak parking lots. The drivers and escorts camped around them. Locals wandered about. We'd deal with reports of runaways the next day, because our disaffected youths could come no closer to joining a travelling circus.

I found my big brother between two tanker trucks. He motioned me over to his tent when he saw me approaching. "Nice digs," I said.

"On the plus side, I have it all to myself."

"One of these your truck?" I asked.

"We alternate, but this one is mine tomorrow. These here carry milk."

"Really- there's a working dairy farm somewhere?" Milk sounded appealing because of its rarity.

"The big world holds more you don't know about. Everything's coming back."

A pair of his fellow convoy guards joined us. They introduced themselves as Hector and Jason. I shared out the croissants. Everybody talked about the great life in Jersey. The power grid had returned. Wind farms brought power back to the easternmost Finger Lakes. I had visions of the undead sweeping across scenic hills against a backdrop of windmills.

They all liked Rochester, but it felt behind the curve, though better off than Syracuse, in a poor compliment. As for their next destination, Buffalo, they grew quiet. None of them liked it there- too many men with too many guns.

Hector punched me in the arm. "I hear little brother doesn't like the big wide world."

"Leave him be," said B. "You haven't walked in his shoes as he hasn't walked in yours."

Jason shrugged, "Isn't so bad out there anymore. It's the regular people who cause more trouble than them walkers."

"People protect what little they have," I suggested.

"You haven't seen it," said Hector. "Greedy bastards are ending up with quite a bit. This whole plague thing didn't turn out too badly for them."

"I thought we had been coming back," I said. "I mean the whole country."

Jason shrugged. "Bleeding hearts in Rochester have no idea. The world is coming back, but it will be a whole different place."

Hector continued, "We're coming back but there are going to be different people in charge. The new currency is land."

"I thought the new currency would be dollars."

"You are so stupid, Jason," said Hector.

"Your mother is stupid."

"No mothers, man. A walker ate mine."

"I had no idea. I'm sorry about...," Hector said.

"Psych out- she's living in Bayonne."

"Might have been better off if a walker had eaten her- I've been to Bayonne," Hector grinned before he looked at me, "Of course, there are still a lot of zeds out there."

"Zeds?" The first time I had heard the term.

"It's what they call them out West," said Jason. "Herds of them wander the prairie like the buffalo used to."

My brother yawned. "Don't pay attention to him. He hasn't been further west than Toledo."

"I met a guy in Binghamton, and he knew stuff. There are tribes of survivors out West, living like settlers. They've all become hunter-gatherers."

Hector interrupted, "And they know how to use every part of the zombie. Nothing goes to waste."

"Fine, forget I said anything," said Jason.

"Zombies roaming the prairies sound pretty bad to me. I read a book once..."

My brother snickered. "You are our intellectual, Hector."

"...about passenger pigeons. There used to be so many of them that a flock flying overhead at noon could block out the sun. Coming to your town they would wipe out all the food and damage buildings and stuff. Of course, we hunted them, and they went extinct, even worse than the buffalo."

"I doubt there are any buffalo left," said B. "I can't see them standing up to a herd of undead."

I left soon after, not terribly interested in contemplating the end of a species.

***

I overslept the next morning. No one owned an alarm clock. We mostly tell time by general acclimation, so I wouldn't be late for work if nobody else thought so.

"You're late," announced Sarge. "We have a corpse walking up the bike path. We have boys out on the bridge. You want to check it out and bring a little mature decision making to the team?"

"I didn't know you thought of me like that, Sarge."

"I wouldn't if half the force didn't oversleep today seeing how they finally had a decent meal. One of the tankers came into town full of beer, damn stupid if you ask me, but I'm impressed it made it this far." He smiled and then refocused his attention on me. "What are you doing standing there?"

I ran from the building and over to the river bridge. Einstein, Conover, McLovin' and Tony stood there, watching something in the distance. McLovin' held the binoculars. Einstein looked through the sights on a rifle. I demanded the binoculars.

"You have to look past those damn zombie pens. They make it blurry," Conover said, "She's dragging her dead self this way. Nobody else is on the path for now."

Einstein offered, "I can hit it in another hundred yards."

"No, you can't," challenged McLovin'.

I tuned out their bickering. "Damn it," I shouted. "I know her. I recognize the clothes."

"They'll be rags soon enough," said Einstein.

"I interviewed her yesterday. Who reported her?"

They all shrugged. I wanted to scream. Through the lenses, I watched Irene stagger.

I shoved the binoculars back at McLovin'. "Keep her in sight." I turned to Conover. "Give me your hammer." He carried it with him everywhere. Staring at me, he withdrew it from his holster. Then he kissed it. Then he passed it to me. I nodded and took off down the road.

Phil saw me coming at a run. A good man, he knew I had a reason and stayed out of my way. Once I hit the top of Mt. Hope, I turned toward the river behind the old cable television building. Unlikely to pick up speed, Irene would still be a distance away, but I wanted to intersect her. I glanced back toward the bridge to see my fellow officers.

They indicated nothing and I headed down the bike path. I slowed to a walk and caught my breath.

Irene came into view, high stepping like the newly turned tend to do. Zombies occasionally have good eyesight and she saw me immediately. She smelled me, because she locked on with the sudden head turn which serves as an early warning system if you're lucky enough to notice. I wanted luck. The last thing we needed would be for her to wander from the river and bite a civilian.

I slowed even more, took out the hammer, and practiced swinging to know the heft of it. Conover had taped the handle. It felt good in my hand. Then I saw the words scribbled on the grip: "Baby Killer." It gave me pause. I didn't need to know the back story.

When I looked up, a mother and child walked around a nearby apartment building and headed for the river. Irene did not groan, and she moved lightly on her feet because the breathers hadn't noticed her yet. Irene noticed them though. I ran and yelled. I brandished the hammer hoping to be clear about my intentions. I shouted, "I'm a police officer," hoping it meant something.

Calm as could be, the mother gently pushed her child behind her and pulled out a handgun. I measured fifty yards away from them and another thirty to Irene. Mom stepped into her firing stance and carefully aimed. I shouted, "Let me!"

Mom fired twice into Irene's chest to slow her down and stand her upright. It resounded like a cannon going off. I pulled up short and bent over gasping for breath. The noise signaled how safe people felt. In the old days, nobody used a gun like it for fear of drawing more zombies. Then mom moved steps closer and put a bullet in Irene's head.

Mom turned to me with a Cheshire Cat smile, "You're welcome."

I pulled myself together and looked at the mess which used to be Irene.

With arms folded across her chest, mom strolled over beside me. "Those hollow point bullets make a tangle, but they do the job."

I mumbled something like, "Yes, ma'am."

"So, you're a cop?" She patted her holstered gun. "Makes you feel useless, doesn't it, when everyone is carrying one of these?"

"Sometimes," I crouched down beside the remains, looking for anything which might hint at Irene's initial cause of death. "Did you know her?" I asked without looking up.

"I'm not sure what you take me for, but I don't know any walkers."

I sighed heavily, "When she lived, ma'am?"

She shifted her weight and peered at Irene, "There aren't a lot of us in the Wedge yet. She looks familiar, but I can't say for sure. Is she new?"

"Recent and she called herself Irene."

"What is it, honey?" Her child stood behind her.

The little one stared at Irene. "She had a pet cat, Mommy."

"You be quiet, honey."

I stayed on my haunches and turned to face the child. "You're right." I positioned myself so she couldn't see the remains. I don't know why. Her eyes had doubtless seen worse. "What's your name?"

"Tracy." She shifted her feet and looked at the ground.

"It's a very pretty name, Tracy. This woman used to be Irene, but she died. Your Mom did what she had to do."

Tracy's mother didn't approve. "I don't think I need you to..."

I interrupted. "Tracy, do you remember the color of Irene's cat?"

"Uh-hunh," She answered, accompanied by more rocking.

"Can you tell me?"

Tracy glanced at her mother who nodded. "Black."

"Good, good." It elicited a big smile from Tracy. I rose to my feet. "Do you live near Alexander Street?" I asked Tracy's mother after taking out a notepad and pencil nub.

She took her turn to sigh. "Yes, in the big brown house with the yellow door."

"Name?"

She looked at her daughter, "Partridge- Shirley Partridge."

She might have joked but I contemplated my feet and the disturbing stains on them. "Your daughter is right. Irene did have a black cat. We would really like to... detain it." I noticed zombie ooze on my pants cuff.

"I bet you would," said Shirley. She looked at Irene. "I suppose it explains how this happened to her. I wouldn't want to think we had a breach in the wall."

"Someone will walk the perimeter and we'll have someone come by the neighborhood. Keep an eye out for a couple of days and report anything at all."

Shirley snorted as she turned to leave, "Yea, right."

I wanted to stop her, but she hadn't done anything.

I heard Tracy asking, "What does detain mean?"

Down river, Einstein and Tony came toward me. I found a bench and waited for them.

"Who saved your ass?"

I glared at Einstein. "I wanted to preserve the body. The way she shot it up, we'll never know what turned her." I looked at the sky. "You guys stay here, and I'll go back to the station. I can send out the pickup crew."

"You don't need to," said Tony. "McLovin' went back soon as we saw the zombie drop. You might as well go back to HQ. You can do the paperwork. We can watch the body until the sanitation boys show up."

Five

"Explain to me again, Crash, how the woman you talked to not twenty-four hours previously became a walker within the walls of our fair city. Run through it one more time for my amusement."

"Sarge, I don't think the cat had anything to do with it."

We sat in his office, the two of us. He looked at me with pity. "Not the cat, you say. How can you be so sure? Did you happen to notice something before one of our local parent activists destroyed all the evidence?"

"No, Sarge."

"Now, son, you and I both know there has been no proof cats or dogs or much else carries the plague." Sarge slammed his hand on a pile of papers. "I am sure I even have an official statement to such effect, but incidents like this don't help. These things lead to hysteria, and you know where hysteria leads?" He leaned back in his chair and rested his feet on the desk.

"No, sir."

"Squirrel hunting, rat baiting, pigeon shoots."

"Sir?" I asked.

"Do you want to be the officer in charge of eradicating squirrels from the city, son? I don't think so."

"No, sir, what about the legs?"

Sarge pulled his feet off the desk. "Are you implying something about my manners, son?"

"No, sir. Irene's legs. We must still have her parts from the chest down. In addition, we have the arms. It's where the cat would have been most likely to scratch her."

"And what would it prove, the cat had claws?" Sarge pitied me. "It means nothing if the deceased didn't transform because of it. You're barking up the wrong tree. How about if we go a little old fashioned?"

"How so, sir?" I asked.

"Investigate further."

"I don't know if I'm cut out for this job, sir. What about Sherlock?" I referred to our legendary detective with an apparently huge ego.

"You know Sherlock hasn't set foot outside the building since last year. He's an old, somewhat damaged man and not going to be stepping out. I need someone quite a bit younger and less prone to disobeying orders." Sarge smiled at me.

***

The next day, I started my new case, though Sarge and I may have been the only ones who knew. I dressed the same because I owned nothing else. Overnight, I dropped by Sherlock's spot in the barracks, but he stayed away. I hoped for advice but ended up curious where an old recluse would be in the dark.

Riding to the South Wedge, I considered what Sherlock would do in my position. I decided he would do nothing, pretty much as he had been for the past year. He hid out on the roof of the station. I hoped I would do better than him after a couple of years as a detective.

Finding the Partridge house proved easier than looking for a yellow door. Shirley had not mentioned the bus, but the sight proved a significant giveaway. The paint had faded, and they had patched windows, but it sat in their front yard. Tracy ran around out front playing with a boy about her size. Before I could approach their home, Shirley came to the street. On her way, she shoo-ed Tracy and the boy inside.

She smiled, "Don't even mention the bus. Everybody asks. We had a large crew to transport and found the bus sitting around. We hid out at the library in Fairport. One of us, maybe me, found this old record player and a bunch of LPs in the back. They hadn't been on the circulation shelves in forever. I doubted they interested anyone. Not the best use of our power, but we had a lot of kids with us and wanted to burn off their energy, so we danced."

"And one of those records happened to be...," I completed the story.

"The Partridge Family Album; one morning, we scavenged and did not find food, but we found paint. David grabbed it," Shirley smiled serenely. "He must have seen a picture of the bus in the library stacks somewhere- maybe the album cover. An old bus had parked in the lot behind the library."

"Amazing it still worked."

Shirley nodded. "When we heard about the Mayor's amnesty, we took our chances in the big city. By then, I found myself the only adult left with five children. David and Susan never had a chance to be children. They live in the bus now."

"They're not really...?"

"Oh, no, it would be weird," Shirley considered. "Maybe not any more...or ever."

The tires on the bus had stopped being round. "The bus doesn't look like it's going anywhere again."

"Yes." We stood in silence, contemplating the last ride of the Partridge family bus. After a respectful moment, she turned to me, "I'd offer you something to drink, but I'm not interested in inviting you in if you're here to harass us."

I tried to smile. "You haven't broken any laws. I came by to ask a few questions."

She considered my words, shrugged, and headed for the front porch. "You might as well sit down. We can spare water."

"I appreciate it." I pushed my bike over to a tree and selected a chair. The weather had stayed nice, and I enjoyed the breeze.

Shirley returned empty handed and sat beside me. "We might have a treat for you. Give Danny a couple minutes."

"All right," I inhaled deeply. "The smell is not too bad today."

She tipped back and forth on a rocker. "The wind is blowing east to west. You don't hear the pit over here either."

"I bet you do at night."

"They're always louder at night," Shirley grimaced. "Tracy wears earmuffs. The rest of us ignore it, I guess."

"Everyone in the city ignores it."

"I don't know why it's there."

A redheaded boy balancing a tray bearing two china cups rescued me from saying something wrong.

I recognized the scent immediately but doubted the truth.

Danny put the tray down on one of the chairs. "We don't have cream, but there's sugar. It's clumpy, but it dissolves if you stir it, and it tastes the same."

I couldn't help myself. "Where did you find coffee?" I knew it could be dangerous to ask about a stash, but certain commodities had become too special.

Danny raised an eyebrow at Shirley.

She patted my arm. "I don't think I'm going to answer, even if you are asking in an official capacity."

"I'm not." I sipped. It tasted like the real thing, but I didn't remember well enough to know.

Danny leaned over and kissed Shirley before bringing the tray back inside-- none of my business and not a question worth my life asking, even more than the one about their coffee cache. Shirley stared hard at me, as if daring me to say something.

Besides, I wanted to finish my drink, "Tastes good." I blew on the top of the cup, even though it felt cool enough. I wallowed in the whole experience. "Did you know Irene, the zombie you shot? She lived a little way down the street." I motioned directionally.

"Sure. As Tracy told you, we knew her because of the cat. I wondered about her living alone. She did, didn't she? Do you need me to look in on someone? Don't tell me she hid children?"

"Never. Have you noticed anything unusual?"

"Since you mention it, it's been noisy the last couple days," said Shirley. "I think it came from her direction."

"Noisy, like how?"

"Like people moving out. People come and go. I try not to put my nose in their business." She held up the coffee cup for a beat too long before taking a sip.

My cup looked empty, even when I tipped it back and licked the rim. "I really appreciate your hospitality. Tell Danny he makes a great cup of coffee."

***

Enough daylight remained, so I went to Irene's old home. The door unlocked, but it meant nothing. Keys had become hard to come by and walkers didn't do well at opening doors. They pushed until the frame gave way. Of course, human miscreants could be a threat. Pre-plague crimes had a habit of making a comeback. While those may have included breaking and entering, other people slept with a gun under their pillow. My current job as a police officer made a comeback because of both sides in such an encounter.

The interior of the house appeared as I had left it. The signs of our struggle remained. Irene didn't have much worth scavenging. She had books, mostly college textbooks. She had hit the science section of the university bookstore hard. All those books piled in one corner and didn't bear the layer of dust which covered everything else.

The stairs to the second floor looked untrodden so I decided Irene hadn't spent much time up there. The rooms smelled ripe. On the plus side, I didn't find any remains or bits and bobs of people. Broken plumbing accounted for most of the stench. The mattresses had rotted. Nothing hid under the beds. One bureau tipped over, but the rest of the furniture sat in place. Irene said this had been her former family home.

The time must have long gone for her family when she returned. I couldn't imagine finding your loved ones had departed without you. Not the only one deserted, Irene would have found the fact cold comfort.

In a universal (and retroactively pointless) effort to increase resale value, homeowners had finished attics across the South Wedge over the last couple of decades. Irene's family fit the profile. I found a locked door behind a bookcase. I listened for a full two minutes and heard no movement. I drew my truncheon, so I felt ready. A much more modern door than the others inside the house meant it would give with a good kick. So, I gave it one.

Immediately, I realized I had mis-blamed the source of the stench edging around my nose. The smell originated upstairs. Irene's family hadn't deserted her as I had concluded, though the effect would have been much the same. They had never turned. Both parents and a younger brother found their final resting place in the attic. They had a final picnic. A radio sat nearby, leaking battery acid. The nauseating smell proved to be old, old booze. The air had mummified the bodies.

The space closed in as I considered the tragic tableau. I made a mental note to send the sanitation crew over when I returned to the station. The house could be redeemed. Nobody needed to know about the previous residents. Every house had its stories, and you'd have to be in serious denial anymore to think the backstories at all pleasant.

Untouched boxes surrounded the bodies in the attic. Someone had carried their mementos up here. A photo lay on the floor among the corpses. It showed a much younger Irene in mortarboard, shining a big smile. Irene must have been living with the fact her family had waited for her, which might have been worse than desertion. In that moment, I changed my mind about the sanitation crew.

Whatever I would do, I wanted to finish searching through the house first. The basement remained. A shiny lock hung on the door. I listened intently at the door and heard nothing. Sanitation had incinerated Irene's body, so I hoped she hadn't been carrying the key. They might have kept it, but I couldn't count on them.

I shifted nearby items and uncovered no key. My luck changed when I reached up and felt along the top of the doorframe, impressed Irene could reach high enough; maybe she used a chair as a boost.

The reek hit me hard. Prepared for the smell of decay and foul flesh on a constant basis, this time I smelled bleach and stood gagging at the top of the stairwell. I saw light filtering through to the basement, but I retrieved my flashlight from my bike anyway, more an excuse for fresh air.

The stairs creaked with age and the walls stood unfinished. Irene used the basement. She had shoved all the original contents of the cellar to one side. Folding tables sat in organized rows now. Laboratory equipment covered every available surface. Irene had been up to more than she let on. I couldn't believe I had sat right overhead without a clue.

With a couple of years of undergraduate science in my background, I recognized most of the equipment, even if I couldn't make it add up to a full laboratory. Vials of compounds sat in one area, so she held chemistry intentions. I recognized a distiller. Multiple microscopes scattered here and there. I decided she had scrounged whatever she could.

An operating table in the farthest corner looked most disturbing of all-- bloodstained, beneath two windows, presumably for the best light. Maybe someone had interrupted Irene. Too small for an adult. No gas tanks for anesthesia. I remembered one of the professors in the lab proposing experimenting on embryos found in female zombies might provide a solution to the plague. Rumors abounded that the few fetuses found had not turned.

Then I remembered the cat. I shone my flashlight into a scattering of buckets and bins, worried about what I might discover. Under a tarp, I uncovered ten or more pet carriers, assorted sizes.

I heard a "meow" upstairs and raced to the first floor. The sound came from the front porch. As soon as I opened the door, the black cat nonchalantly crossed the threshold and headed for the bedroll. I made my second major decision of the day then. I would not kill this cat and would do my best to make sure no one else did either. Unconvinced it had mattered to Irene, it mattered to me. Sometimes you must save something, anything.

***

"What do you mean you had a cup of coffee?" I faced Sarge in his office. I had mostly reported my activities for the day, and he had picked out the most important detail immediately.

"At the Partridge place, the boy brought it out to us on the porch."

"Danny? The smart-ass adolescent, right?" recalled Sarge.

"I believe so. The version I met didn't have as much to say."

"So, they have coffee. Did you ask where they found it?"

"She evaded my inquiry."

"Well, the Mayor will have my ass if we don't find out. You can leave it in my hands." Sarge leaned forward. "You think this Dixon woman engaged in science shenanigans?"

"Dickinson, sir. She filled her basement with laboratory equipment. I have no idea what she had in mind, but it certainly looked like something out of order."

"I thought you had been a scientist in the past life," said Sarge.

"Never graduated, and this looked like a mix of something out of a mad scientist movie or an ER."

"Well, you're the detective. What's your next step?" asked Sarge.

I didn't feel flattered. I felt like I stepped out on a tree limb and waved back at Sarge, safely secured close to the trunk. "I should spend more time nosing around Irene's neighborhood. Maybe even spend a night in the house."

"Too good for the barracks, are you?" Sarge smiled.

"No, sir, but certain things only happen at night. I don't believe that I'm the only one interested in Irene."

Sarge rose from his chair. "Hunches will do you well in this job, especially since evidence is going to be hard to find." He patted me on the back. "I appreciate the way you brought the coffee to me, son. Let's keep it between us. I don't want someone trying to make a name for themselves and stirring up trouble."

***

That night, I went in search of Sherlock again without any luck initially. I followed one of those hunches Sarge encouraged and headed for the roof. Suddenly I batted one thousand because I found the old man doing the slowest dance ever seen. "Are you doing tai chi?"

He smirked at me but said nothing.

"Sarge tells everyone you used to be a detective, a good one. He tells me I'm the new one in the department. This case I'm on- I have hunches, but nothing concrete. I hoped to pick your brain."

Sherlock finished whatever he had been doing and grabbed a nearby towel. "Congratulations, Detective Crash. In your shoes, I would cease saying 'pick your brain' considering the world surrounding us."

I asked, "Why do you do this stuff?"

"You mean the tai chi?"

"Are you a Buddhist or something?"

"You imply I believe in something," said Sherlock. "I do it because it settles my mind. If you're a detective, then you might think about what settles your mind, especially if you're going to rely on hunches."

"I don't see how I have a choice. Our CSI capabilities are limited these days."

"Don't let the walkers take away your intelligence before they consume your brain," said Sherlock. "You can still look for clues. Evidence is the basis of police work. Hunches will only lead you down the wrong path."

"How can I look for evidence where there isn't any? The victim turned into a zombie. A shooter obliterated her remains. We cremated the rest. I have no witnesses. I have no motive for her death except she did experiments no one knew anything about."

"You know about them now," Sherlock pointed out.

"Because I broke into her basement."

"See, you sought evidence. You're already acting like a detective. Now think like one."

***

I spent the next morning figuring out which tools of my new trade might be handy. I loaded a backpack and wheeled my bike out of the barracks.

Before I walked five yards, Sarge came up behind me and put his arm across my shoulders. "It's your lucky day, son." It sounded like the opposite. "The Mayor wants to see us. Bring the bike. The Mayor's place has wonderful guards who will watch it very carefully."

We strolled in silence for a block. The sky hung heavy and dark, like most days in Rochester. We had experienced a good run of sun, but it would become a memory. The wind picked up and the air smelled like wet zombies, a tang which never becomes normal.

"Is this about the coffee?" I ventured.

He evaded. "You spoke with Sherlock. He thinks you might be all right."

It didn't feel like a compliment. We arrived at the Mayor's offices after a few more minutes of moody quiet. The Mayor had re-purposed one of the buildings by the High Falls. He kept an entourage of family and guards and bureaucrats. The building loomed large. Littered with bedrolls and supplies, many folks had developed a need for the proximity to power and any closeness, especially at night. I lived in a barracks, so I inhabited no position to judge.

The building had housed restaurants and nightspots in better years. Of the three main doors on the street, debris blocked one and guards at the second sent us to the third. A giant of a man took my bike and backpack and assured me I would have them back. A second guard, smaller than the first, frisked us and took our guns. He didn't say anything about returning them, but we assumed.

A teenager ran out as we went in. Everyone in the city knew a steady flow of runners passed between the Mayor's office and the library. As a decent job for anyone quick enough, potential replacements competed every summer in a variety of contests.

Once inside, the lack of tech startled me. Using pen and paper, the bureaucrats sat behind mostly empty desks. The lucky few had staplers and rulers. I saw two calculators and three slide rules, and one woman had an abacus. Only three blocks away sat high-powered computers and telecommunications.

No one nudged us along or offered directions. Unless we wanted to spend the day among the accountants, we had to find a way through the paper-pushing herd. I headed for a doorway to the far left, but Sarge grabbed my arm and pointed toward the back of the room. Glass windows filled the entire rear wall. With his back to us, leaning on a railing, a large man stood outside.

We found a door when a guard stopped us as we set foot on the back patio. The Genesee River cascaded over the High Falls, cutting a huge gash in the earth beyond the railing. The view inspired awe, but two goons distracted us because they pressed their hands into our chests and frowned meaningfully.

"Move it or lose it," muttered Sarge.

The goon prepared to let Sarge try until the Mayor spoke. "Let them approach." His voice always threw me- too musical, too high for such a large man. Large like someone who used to be all muscle and slowly added more layers... a strategic geological weight gain.

The Mayor, the two goons, Sarge and I left space on the porch. The wind blew strong above the chasm. The miasma which hovered in the air downtown had gone undetectable.

The Mayor dragged his right hand across his baldpate, sighed, turned around slowly, and talked. "I saw my first zombie down there on the bridge. The Genesee brewery at the other end opened a restaurant. Four of us from Midtown came over after spending the morning at the athletic club. We sat outside.

"I saw the beast in the distance coming across the bridge, no idea what I looked at. A family stood halfway across, admiring the view. The father must have figured it out, because he placed himself in the creature's path as it veered toward his children. I saw it bite him. He wrestled with it... punched-- they struggled. For your loved ones, it's amazing what a person can do. The father threw the zombie off the bridge. His wife screamed. She looked horrified.

"I've often wondered what happened to the family. Without a doubt, the father had been infected. In the ensuing days, mom saw worse things than a zombie tossed off a bridge."

He turned to face us. Always difficult to look the Mayor in the face, his left cheek absent, prompting many stories and he denied none of them. "I think about that family every day, but I don't often think about absent friends. I know they're dead. When we blocked the bridge days later to keep the zombies on their side of the river, I wonder what my friends might think about what I've accomplished."

Sarge went and stood by the railing. "People have lives they never thought possible again. It's because of what we've accomplished."

"Did you know zombies can cross water? They walk along the bottom." The Mayor seemed incapable of keeping a train of thought on a straight track.

Sarge motioned toward me. "The boy knows more science stuff."

The Mayor moved over beside Sarge and suddenly slapped him on the back. "We old warriors have to stick together! How are things at the police department?"

"Well, Your Honor, I wanted you to meet our newest detective."

"Probably wise giving up on the agoraphobe," The Mayor eyed me from bottom to top. "You must have the brains in the department. Excellent! We need brains. What have you been detecting for us? I hope nothing too heinous is going on in my city."

I tried to speak, but Sarge spoke for me. "He's made an interesting discovery. He has uncovered coffee."

"You don't say. Now you have something worth looking into." He strode over to me and stood too close. Then he sniffed me. I had to fight every reflex not to cringe. "I like him, Sarge. Let's see if we can keep this one on the job."

"Will do, Your Honor."

His Honor considered me like he might a zombie which he needed to know how best to take out quickly. "What do you like, detective?"

I stared back blankly. Thinking about what you like had long been an effort doomed to end in depression.

"Come on, boy." The Mayor bellowed magnanimously. "What will it be? Cigarettes? Caffeine pills? Shampoo? Beer? Fine! If you can't think of anything, then go inside and ask Sharon to give you something."

At a nod from the Mayor, one of the goons took my arm and led me back inside. He pointed at a woman in a red dress at the far end of the room. The crowded space felt oppressive after the porch. I wove between desks and filing cabinets. Sharon sat in a makeshift sitting room. It had no walls, but a sofa and two armchairs rested on a carpet. She appeared engrossed in a pile of papers before her on a coffee table. After all my weaving, I leaned against the nearest wall and waited for her to look up. Finally, she did, "Yes?"

"The Mayor sent me to you? He said to ask you for something."

She had long hair tied into a ponytail. You did not see long hair much anymore. Nobody wanted to give a zombie anything extra to grab onto. Sharon wore glasses, which meant she had luck finding a pair which fit and improved her vision. Also, she wore a red dress. No one had ever said the dead must be color blind, but current preferences suggested everyone felt bright colors attracted walkers.

"Swell," Sharon sounded tired. "Did you have anything in mind? What's your pleasure?"

The Mayor (and everyone else) made it sound harder to come by alcohol than the reality. "Can you arrange computer time? On the net?"

Sharon laughed at me. "Even if I wanted to, the geeks don't share. Look around you. Do we look like we have the tech time we want? They keep telling the Mayor electricity is limited and he's too afraid to argue in case they do something stupid, and it all goes to shit again."

"How about chocolate? Any lying around?"

"Let me take a look." Sharon withdrew a key she had hidden beneath her top. Two guards let her pass and unlock a door I hadn't noticed before. Struggling to look tough or at least competent in front of the muscle, I waited for her. As I decided to make conversation with her guards, Sharon returned. "It's your lucky day." She held out two chocolate bars from the old Niagara confectioner. "We found cases lying around in the schools. Don't think for a moment there's anymore where those came from."

"Thank you."

We stood awkwardly until she waved her hand at me to leave. Fortunately, Sarge returned. He whistled across the room. "Let's go, kid!"

Once outside, we grabbed our things without trouble. A queue had developed while we did our business inside. The line stretched halfway down the block.

"Glad we showed up early," commented Sarge. "The Mayor holds an open house twice a week. I can't imagine what any of them hope to accomplish since he's a nut job and a figurehead." I glanced at him. "Don't look at me like I spoiled Christmas. The techs run the city and you'd know it if you took a moment to think. Considering the shape of things, survival and civilization depend on organization. Why are you staring at me with your mouth hanging open?"

"I can't remember the last time you put so many words together. I didn't know you thought about these things."

"I'm like those other idiots in the department? Nobody made it this far without thinking. Folks stopped when they saw the dark pit at the end of all these thoughts. Most live in the moment and others decided to leave the thinking to somebody else, like the Mayor."

"I'm sorry, Sarge."

"Don't be stupid, son. Only open your eyes. You're a detective now so you need to act like one." We stood outside the barracks. He finally noticed my gear on the bike. "You look packed for a camping trip."

"I might spend the night in the Wedge."

"The pleasures of serious police work. Don't put yourself in excessive danger."

Six

I pulled my bandanna over my mouth and nose as I crossed into the South Wedge. Anyone who believed the infection carries through the air must have lost their mind by now because I don't know where you can go outside without the whiff of decay. You heard rumors of bunkers and shelters deep underground, but I couldn't imagine it was a better life than this one.

I passed the Partridge homestead on my way to Irene's former abode. The house across the street from the band bus has new occupants. I recognize the representatives of the state in search of secret coffee reserves. In the early days of the Mayor, he asked everyone to turn in high-value commodities voluntarily. As the city gained more definition, the surrender of items like coffee, chocolate, and tobacco became a requirement of residence. While holdouts and hoarders happened, we have uncovered most in the ensuing years.

I imagined most hoarders don't have anything left even if they managed to avoid scrutiny. Not after your child's last peanut butter cup, the Mayor did want the case of chocolate chips you grabbed from the grocery store during a food riot. The administration stored the goods in a building near the Mayor's place and handed them out on special occasions.

At Irene's, the front door hung open. People may not employ locks, but no one who lived through the plague could see a swinging door and not feel a rising fight-or-flight reaction. I pulled out my flashlight and gun. I didn't need them given the sunlight as well as the general safety of the neighborhood. The danger would be looters. Word travels fast.

I sniffed and didn't notice the tang of the undead. I stuck my head through the doorway and saw the intruder in the old dining room. Her back to me, engrossed in the pile of books before her, I stepped quietly and entered the house fully.

"You're never going to sneak up on anyone with heavy feet. I didn't make it this long without being able to pay attention to two things at once." She turned around. "Look who it is- my old friend from the ration line."

I lowered my gun. "They aren't rations. They're..."

"Don't go all Orwell on me, Officer Cash. I will only think less of you and then I might become sarcastic."

"Who are you?"

"Call me Frida."

"Like the painter?"

"It's nice to know your college education didn't go to waste." Frida frowned. "I don't suppose I could lower my hands."

"What are you doing here?"

"I knew Irene," said Frida. "I heard what happened and figured I'd drop by."

"Lower your hands. You're claiming her stuff?"

"I can't say nice Irene had anything I actually want," said Frida. "I needed to see what could turn her into one of them in a safe neighborhood. Doesn't it seem odd to you?"

"I came out here the other day because she kept a cat."

Frida's skepticism showed.

"I know," I agreed. "I don't believe it's transmitted by living animals either, but it is oddly coincidental."

"I agree with you," said Frida, "but not for the same reasons."

I let it go. "The cat has gone missing, so we'll never know." I had to justify myself. "I visited here yesterday. Irene had been through serious stuff."

"Who hasn't?" Frida's chin stuck out. "You gave the place a once over? Are you a detective now? Not a bouncer for His Honor the Mayor?"

"As a matter of fact...," I stopped in mid-sentence. I didn't want to continue the argument. I changed tracks, instead. "You look like you tried doing a little detective work yourself? What's your interest? You're behaving like more than a friend."

"Fine, I used to write for the Democrat and Chronicle," said Frida.

"I heard newspapers are a dying medium." I turned and walked through the house looking for whatever Frida might have touched.

Frida followed. "I didn't say I'm in my dream job, but we did have a line on the news when things went to shit. We had as good a seat as anyone in Rochester when the President and everyone failed. I remember the day the Speaker took over. I shouldn't have been in shock. Once those damn things snuck in somewhere, people waited for the lights to turn out. Washington might not have been first worldwide, but the first on the east coast."

"I remember. Why'd you pull all these books out?" I asked.

"Why didn't you?"

"Answer the question. This will be easier if you do."

"I doubt it," Frida said. "They're notebooks and I wondered what they contained."

"What did you find?"

Frida looked at me disdainfully. "They're notes on experiments, but I can't make sense of them."

I went to the pile Frida had made and glanced through the pages. "These are all in different handwriting. They can't all be Irene. I think they might be from the same Chemistry 101 class."

"You might not be utterly useless."

"I'm sorry. Did you happen to say what you do nowadays?" I asked.

"I'm still a reporter. Now it's broadsheets."

"That's you?" I had seen them on lampposts and walls. They became our new newspapers. Radio might be on the comeback and appeared likely to alter things again.

"We have a full staff," said Frida.

"You're funded by the Mayor."

"Not exactly- more like he tolerates us. We have friends in tech plaza, though."

"And you think Irene might be fodder for the broadsheets?" I asked.

"It's not why I'm here."

I had my doubts. "Have you been in the basement?" Someone left the door slightly ajar. I pushed it open all the way.

"It's a little strange down there," said Frida.

Leading the way with my flashlight, we descended the steps. I wanted to know what Frida made of all the equipment. Someone had shifted things. I assumed the culprit had to be Frida.

She commented, "Irene must have been up to something weird."

I agreed as I shone the light around the room, highlighting each table in turn.

Frida had more thoughts however, "Seriously- you make nothing more of this?"

"How else do you explain it?" I asked.

"Look closer. Does any of it make sense?" she wondered. "Her stuff is broken. I see bits and pieces, but nothing functional. The centrifuge doesn't have a motor. It looks like a movie set."

Feeling stupid and confused, I let the light go out. Then I shuffled over to the nearest table. With the light back, I could see Frida had it right. Why hadn't I noticed? "You knew Irene? What do you make of this setup?"

"I can't say for sure," said Frida. "It's not like it functioned."

"She might have been assembling a lab and never finished."

"Really- and what did she aim to do? Stand over bubbling colored water and cackle?"

"What about the cat?" I asked. "Maybe she wanted to do something with it?"

Frida laughed sadly, "Yea, Irene the vivisectionist. It looks possible, but not if you use your brains."

"This mishmash is a bother to go to for no reason. Irene is dead and someone filled her house with junk. Why? Are they even related?"

We went upstairs. Why would someone foil a police inquiry when hardly anyone investigated murder cases? They needn't have on my account. I looked at Frida. Could she be the reason or the perpetrator? "There's something you're not telling me."

"Imagine a mountain with a giant cave filled with filing cabinets," answered Frida. "Those cabinets contain all the things I know which you don't."

I knew her type and, despite it, I asked the question any sane person never bothered to ask anymore. The very act of mouthing the words inevitably let someone else's crazy run free. "Why don't you enlighten me?"

Frida's tone became even more patronizing. "Did Irene tell you anything about herself?"

"We attended the U. of R. at the same time. We both did the sciences. She didn't tell me much more, but I learned a little looking around here."

Frida considered her next few words. "How much do you know about how the plague originated?"

Now I knew the particular flavor of this crazy. "Merely the usual rumors, I know nothing for certain."

"Deep thinkers believe it originated in a test tube. They might think the test tube existed here in Rochester. Irene may have been in the laboratory where it happened."

"And you think it has something to do with her death?" I asked.

"I know the world is much stranger than is dreamed of in your petty philosophy."

"What do you know about Irene's family?"

"Not much," said Frida. "They lived here, though I didn't know the exact house until she moved in."

"Did she have siblings?" I more than suspected the answer.

"She mentioned a little brother. I think the worst had happened to him, as well as her parents."

"Did she mention they died in the attic?" I led Frida up the stairs. Those of us who survived the last few years knew how to deal with certain situations which would have defied our younger selves. Frida and I worked respectfully. A shed in the backyard contained tarps and shovels.

We carried Irene's family outside and buried them in shallow graves near the shed. Frida crossed herself over them. I bowed my head and wished for a better world as an improvement over the stream of curses I directed at God when I stood beside gravesites during recent years.

I might be coming to terms with things.

We went inside. Wordlessly, Frida made tea. We sat at the table and shared a bag of stale oyster crackers from her backpack. "What's your next step, detective?"

"I think I'm going to spend the night here. I'd like to find her cat. What about you? Are you going to nose around in Irene's death?"

Frida sipped noisily. "I know a guy at the university, still plugging away in the labs."

"Would he remember Irene?" I asked.

"I think so. It's the lab where she hid for three years. I can take you to him. I wouldn't try popping up on him without me. He acted a little jumpy the last time I visited."

"Are you a friend of his?"

***

I spent the next hour resting after Frida left. I had a sandwich from the police commissary and a handful of Thelma's bland biscuits. She called them scones, but she played fast and loose with too many happy memories. I washed it down with a jug of river water. The sun had set, signaling the time for my second reason for being in the South Wedge. I headed around behind the house and snuck through the backyards.

The Partridge family boundary sat a couple hundred yards away. Bushes had gone wild, and grass had grown hideously, so it took fifteen minutes while nature scratched my legs to bits. Skulking about in the dark had become an effective way to find a bullet in your head, especially on a moonless night. For all my trouble, I should have decided what course of action I planned to follow. Mainly, curiosity (and doubtlessly stupidity) powered me.

"Hey!" hissed a shadow by their house.

The last thing you want to do in a world of zombies is play dumb. It is extremely important to establish your bona fides as quickly as possible, "Person here."

A young man came out of the darkness. He had dark hair and looked as skinny as a Hollywood actor. "Shit, you scared the piss out of me. You're the cop who hung around earlier."

"You have pretty good night vision," I said.

"Yea, it's saved my ass a few times."

"You must be David?"

"I must be."

It felt strange and nice to shake hands, a ritual lost and reclaimed.

"So, why are cops spying on us from across the street?" David asked.

"Who says cops are across the street?"

"I had an unusual upbringing before everything went down. Cops still act like cops. It's reassuring."

"The Mayor wants your coffee." I would never be particularly good at politics.

"Not cool," said David. "I told Shirley we'd be better off outside the fences. The Mayor is a real jerk. We found the coffee ourselves, right here in the neighborhood."

"You mean you didn't bring it into the city from outside? If you stayed outside the fences, then you wouldn't have the coffee either."

He looked at me like I had confirmed my low aptitude. "So?"

"Never mind. If those cops decide it's time, then they're going to come storming into your place and take whatever they want. People will get hurt."

David pulled his gun out of his skinny jeans. "Damn straight."

I pointed his gun toward the ground. "But we don't want that, not over coffee beans. Besides, they might take more than the coffee."

Concentration sketched his face into a variety of expressions. He bore no resemblance to David Cassidy, but I wondered about his singing voice. He interrupted my reverie. "We ought to ask Shirley."

We entered the house through a back door he locked behind us. Soon as he threw the bolts, his body sagged. I sympathized. "Not easy going outside in the dark."

"Not easy going out alone," David added.

We went down a hallway and found Shirley in the kitchen. She sat reading a book by candlelight, smiled at us, and waved the book. "I never lost the habit when we left the library. I do miss having the collection at my fingertips."

"The cop says they want our coffee," stated David.

Shirley slowly lowered the book. "They do? And did he come here to take it?"

I coughed, "No, ma'am. Police officers are across the street. They want your coffee. I'm not with them. I am an officer, but I followed a cat in your backyard when your boy found me."

"You expect me to believe you happen to be in my house while your buddies sit across the street planning a raid?"

At the next moment, David won my unending gratitude. "I believe him, Shirl. He didn't snoop as much as cross the property."

Shirley sighed. "I can't believe I am sitting here after everything which has happened and I'm thinking 'oh, sure, Shirley, he's a cop-they are good people.' Why should I think anything of the kind any-more?"

"I don't know. I am trying, but I don't know how to define a good person nowadays. I'd appreciate it if it meant you didn't shoot me or one of them."

"Relax, officer. Nobody's shooting anybody if I have anything to say about it." She fiddled with her book. "This Mayor wants the coffee and not the boys in blue?"

I nodded.

"No scenario ends with them leaving without a significant contri-bution to the Mayor's coffee coffers. It's only a question of it ending with or without violence?" asked Shirley.

"It sounds about right," I agreed.

"And, right now, they're only interested in our coffee?"

I nodded again.

"What if we told them we didn't have any left?" asked David.

"They'd come in and make sure."

David whined, "Even if we didn't have any left, we'd have to find coffee."

Shirley raised her hand. "Let's not worry about it yet. How much coffee would it take to buy off the Mayor?"

"You can't negotiate with him," I said. "Whatever you have he wants to share."

She grimaced. "It's not completely accurate, but I see your point."

The cops assigned to watch the Partridge place did not do a quality job. David, Danny, and I left through the back door and crossed dark backyards, passing Irene's place. We made noise, but years of sneaking practice stood us in good stead. Danny led us to an old coffee shop at the end of the block. Long ago, the living and the dead smashed the windows. People boarded the holes over. A fence enclosing an outdoor patio remained. The door lay on the ground.

David switched on his flashlight and made a quick scan. Previous visitors had thoroughly looted the main floor. The counter remained, but the raiders made off with the furniture. Additional survivors had scavenged for wood and cloth, leaving the space looking like every other desolate restaurant, café, and bar.

Danny grabbed a metal rod off the floor and went to a door along one wall. It clearly led to the basement. The door must have jammed because he spent minutes prying it open carefully. Lighting the path, David led the way down. The musty smell hit me first. Then, I saw the large sacks piled against the walls. I must have gasped.

"I know," said Danny.

David said, "I figure people must have been too scared to come down here. We had to clear out rats and a single damaged walker."

Danny snickered, "Not exactly a walker- more like a crawler."

"Is it all coffee? And it hasn't gone bad?" I asked.

"A bit of it's a little moldy. We ought to move it to a drier location, but it's heavy and we don't want people to see us hauling all this down the street."

I plopped down on a sack pile. They did the same.

Danny crossed his arms. "I don't want to give it all up to the Mayor. We found it."

I shrugged. "I suppose the question is whether or not it's yours to keep."

David said, "It's about whether or not they'll take it and what we can do about it."

"What about turning over a portion?" I suggested.

In the end, we followed my suggestion. Danny had overseen the stash and he identified ten good sacks which we carried over to Irene's place and put in the attic. We didn't want to hide them at the Partridge place since the police would search it, and we couldn't leave the beans anywhere around the coffee shop for the same reason.

Exhausted when we finished, the boys went home to sleep. They elected me to negotiate the surrender of the remaining coffee with the cops across the street. That could wait until morning. I knew better than to test their ability to differentiate me from a threat if I approached in the dark.

In the morning, I headed across the street first thing. Sarge had assigned Einstein, Jackson Pollack, and Spuds. They acted excited about the coffee lode until they needed to transport it downtown.

I spent the next two days at Irene's house. Susan Partridge brought me over stew for dinner on the first night. As opposed to the others, she looked like her namesake, but I could have been wrong. I remembered long brown hair and big eyes and not a lot more. Susan did not stay and did not say much. I found silverware in Irene's kitchen and ate the food, vegetarian and spicy, over rice. I had eaten similar from many strangers' hands.

On the second morning, I retrieved the cleanest pet crate from the basement. While down there, I uncovered the casement windows and let a little light shine in. Frida had been right. The space looked like a jumble of useless odds and ends, only working as set dressing because of the poor lighting. The days of CSI might be long gone, but I longed for rudimentary fingerprinting capability. Even if I had known how to lift them off the junk, I had no database for comparison.

Beneath a blanket, the pet crate sat on the floor. It did not look like it arrived with the faux lab furnishings. I grabbed the carrier and the blanket and brought them upstairs to the back porch. The air still smelled moist in the late morning quiet. I shook out the dusty blanket, but the crate had fared better. It had held a dog, cat, or whatnot. I folded the blanket, placed it inside the carrier, and left the whole thing open on the back porch. Then I went inside and took a nap.

Still daylight when I awoke, I checked on the pet crate expectantly but met disappointment. I had no idea what the black cat could tell me anyway. I decided the whole endeavor led nowhere. I went inside and packed up my few items. I rode my bike back downtown.

Phil oversaw his post at the bridge. "You missed Einstein and his boys," Phil offered. "They passed back and forth carrying the good stuff. They mentioned you in passing and said to keep an eye out."

"Mighty nice of them," I agreed.

"They said you had looked into the death of the poor crazy cat lady who turned the other day," said Phil.

"I am."

"I don't understand why one death matters so much." His gaze passed over the edge of the bridge to the cages below. "I don't imagine you're going to look into everybody who's passed over in the last few years."

Not entirely sure of the direction of the conversation, I rested my hand on his shoulder. "I am not going to be making anything better about the past, but I can try to help with the present and the future a little bit."

Phil raised his rifle and carefully aimed at one of the zombies down below. "Pow," he hissed. Before this moment, I would have described him as one of the few even-keeled people I knew. As he lowered the rifle, his expression returned to normal. "You ain't been bit while you were outside the city limits proper, I suppose?"

"I've only been in the Wedge, Phil."

"I know, I know, but they have me asking now, probably because of the one you killed by the river."

"I didn't kill it, because someone else did before I arrived." I regretted saying it as soon as the words left my mouth. Everyone knew how Phil felt.

His eyes went blank for a moment. "All right, then, you're good to go. Enjoy the city."

"Thanks, Phil. One day at a time, friend." My feet dragged as I pushed my bike the remaining way across the bridge.

I stopped by the station and asked Sarge about obtaining actual detective tools. He asked me if I thought we had moved beyond the dark ages yet and I had to admit I did not think so.

***

Back in the barracks, the radio station featured the greatest hits of disco. McLovin' freaked out during the night and a couple of the bigger boys locked him in a sedan until he wore himself out.

***

I rode the bike north in the morning. Seneca Park sat up Joseph and along the river above the falls. Still beautiful, it reminded me of a lost world of peaceful nature.

Every now and then, the force did a sweep through the woods looking for anything walking which should not be. I participated in one of those swings in my first week. Sarge had me trailing him, as a new recruit. He took out a doe because anything moving scared us. I stopped him from killing its fawn. We found help at the zoo, since it crested the nearby hill.

Dr. Darwin knew me as the person who brought in the fawn, and she made time for me. She ran the zoo with plenty of help. Now the destination for everyone's pets, you had to volunteer time if you didn't want Rover put down.

The dogs and cats crowded the African safari area toward the back of the grounds. The elephants and other animals who used to live there had lost out to the zombies. Anything unprotected inside one of the main buildings had escaped or died. The big cats, rhinos, alligators, and elephants had not gone down without a fight. Dr. Darwin had hidden in the main house, somehow surviving in the middle of the zombie hurricane.

I found her holding a hedgehog and sitting on a bench inside the entrance. She looked at me with her one good eye. She wore a patch and I constantly reminded myself not to make pirate jokes.

She held out the hedgehog and encouraged me to rub its belly. I swear the little fellow giggled. Doctor Darwin told me new admissions had slowed to a trickle. People would donate most all the cats and dogs that they likely would.

She assumed frightened owners hid a few or put down the rest. "The zombies have wreaked havoc with the fauna of this world," she added. "I hate to contemplate what we have lost around the globe. I know we don't have news from other continents, but the devastation to wild populations must be awful. No lion or elephant or anything is prepared to deal with the undead."

I asked, "What happens to those lions and elephants when bitten? Do we end up with zombie lions? It sounds worse than what's already out there."

Darwin pursed her lips. "Understand that for many species, I have only anecdotal evidence to go on, but it seems to vary. Few animals are susceptible to surviving the infection. I don't have the staff to pursue any full-scale experimentation and too little information to make a reasonable hypothesis."

"I'm not going to let you off so easy. I have a cat on the loose in the South Wedge and people are concerned."

Darwin shrugged. "Look, I didn't work at the zoo before all this. I visited with my daughter on a sunny day. I muted my phone, so I didn't hear the calls from my husband or anyone else. Someone should have made an announcement over the loudspeaker, but I became friends with those people in the weeks and months to follow.

"They had no idea what to announce. How do you tell people the apocalypse has arrived during a rare cloudless day? I always wondered how you don't, but I couldn't retroactively fix it. We found out when we hit the parking lot. I put my daughter in her car seat. We pulled out and then they appeared. I thought I looked at injured people. I couldn't run them over then. I learned to, but I couldn't then."

She took a breath. Looking at me, the gears in her mind shifted. "What I am trying to say is I am a physician. I'm not a vet. We lost the vet the first week and none of his backups ever showed up. I've lived here at the zoo for years. I haven't set foot outside the gate since... My daughter has grown up here. I don't know enough about veterinary medicine to tell you anything for certain."

I grumbled.

"I can tell you I have never seen any feline species turn. None of the tigers or panthers turned. The same goes for all the cats people bring in. They all die when infected and they stay dead. We burn them like the rules say, but it's more to stop the disease we suspect they carry from spreading than anything else."

"What about other species?" I asked.

"We've all heard about the cows." She shrugged.

"And the pigs."

She repeated me. "If I had to guess, it affects the creatures human beings prefer to eat. At least the ones people here in the west have grown fond of."

I gave her as hard a look as I could manage. "Have you ever seen a cow turn?"

Her one good eye did not blink. "I can honestly tell you I have never seen anything not human turn into one of those zombies. And I have seen a lot of different things die."

"Then what are we afraid of? Why go to all this trouble with everybody's pets? It doesn't make sense. Why not leave a little comfort?"

She held out the hedgehog to me. "I know, officer." I took the little creature as she stood and walked back through the zoo. "I want to show you something."

Society had not recovered enough that families would make zoo outings. The pathways stayed empty, "Who could possibly benefit from all these rumors?"

She smiled at me like a mother who learned to encourage without any reason to encourage anyone anymore. "You're overthinking this." Of course, she wanted to use logic. She had hung onto it through all the illogicality of the recent past. "It only takes one story to get around, and people react in the worst conceivable way. I know this may be an unfair comparison, but the McCarthy hearings told one false story which went viral."

"This is zombie cats though."

"Why not communist cats, officer?" she asked as we descended to the old African savannah area. Long empty, Darwin had subdivided the baboon pens for dogs. Most lived in packs, but a couple of incorrigibles lived fenced off to themselves. "Remember how I said I had no scientific proof the pets are safe? Well, I have enough experience with gravity to trust things are going to stick to the ground."

We paused by the glass wall and looked in at the dogs. A teenage girl walked among the beasts passing out chow. Every two steps she stopped and knelt. Each dog had its moment with her. A couple had the crazy look, but it passed soon as she focused on them. From the Rottweilers to the Chihuahuas, they all waited their turn. "I believe you know my daughter, Teresa."

Seven

"So, the cat didn't do it."

Frida nodded. She had sent a note via messenger boy inviting me to breakfast. I suggested MLK Park and brought muffins. Today the bakery flavored them with black pepper. I chose to like them. Frida brought water. "So, you think animals don't carry the disease because a crazy scientist lets her beloved daughter play with puppies?"

"First off, I didn't say they don't carry the disease. Typhoid Mary carried her disease. She didn't suffer from it. Animals can carry it. At least reasonable people have reported it. The animals don't turn, probably."

"So, a dog bite or a cat scratch can still do it?" queried Frida.

"I don't know... maybe." For a proto-scientist, I had not thought this through. I had doubts about Doctor Darwin too.

"Such a tragedy," Tragedy sat on the other side of Frida. Did he mean animals or the empty cup before him?

Frida smiled and poured more water.

He nodded and drank up.

"What do you think, Tragedy? About people being afraid of their pets?" Frida asked, already expecting the usual answer from him.

He squinted into the morning sun. The thin lines around his eyes mapped the hard path which had led him to this moment. Tragedy raised his hand to shield the blinding rays. Then he rose to his feet, dumping muffin crumbs and water on the concrete. With his back to us, he gave off a huge shrug and wandered away.

To Frida's curious glance, I said, "He's not a seer or even a magic eight ball. Maybe he didn't appreciate the expectation."

"I'm not asking for a prognostication!" Frida yelled in his direction. "I wanted to involve him in the conversation."

My turn for a curious glance. In our new world of unusual choices, nobody yelled at Tragedy.

Frida looked embarrassed. With her shoe, she pushed Tragedy's spilled crumbs around. "I know. It's Irene sinking her teeth in me."

We watched the sky and chewed. At night, you could see so many more stars than in my youth. The daytime sky had not changed as much. Still, I enjoyed watching the clouds drift past. "You wanted to meet for breakfast?" I broke the calm.

"Yea and it is about Irene." She ate a little more and I waited. "I can take you to see her former professor, the one she still worked with."

"Really?" Showing the newness of my job, I modulated my tone. "All right, when can we see the guy?"

"He's still at the university along the river," said Frida.

"It's within the Wedge walls nowadays. Where do you want to meet?"

"When did you last set foot on campus?"

I thought back to the day I could not hide from any longer. Voices called out behind me as I ran. I never looked back. "It's been a while."

***

Before my promotion to detective, I had been Sarge's errand boy. I had not done much patrolling in months. In many ways, the promotion solidified my position. Other cops had been Sarge's errand boy, but only Sherlock had ever lasted long enough to become detective. All things considered, it might not be a wise career or life move.

After our trip to see the Mayor, Sarge stayed away from me except to share the administration's gratitude for my role in the acquisition of the coffee. The assumption of graft meant the gratitude had little to no tangible value. On the other hand, maybe Sarge would leave me alone with my investigation. I left a note stating I would spend a few days in the Wedge.

Madge in the cafeteria prepared a backpack of supplies for me. The cooks scrounged up travel meals for all of us. Madge usually threw in a couple books and three cookies. We had three barracks scattered across the city, plus multiple outposts where we rotated men in and out every three or four days.

I snuck a peek in my backpack as I left the station. Someone had been talking because I saw a couple dogeared Rex Stout mysteries sitting right on top of a pile of opaque plastic containers. The two paperbacks smelled of goulash and other people's backpacks.

The wind blew strong and musty, making the air foul. I expected worse south of the pens. We only had one outpost in the Wedge, and I already had a better place to stay. I knew the recently coined adage "A man who sleeps alone wakes up gnawing a bone," but I had confidence in my own health and the safety of Irene's house. I pulled my kerchief over my mouth and nose as I approached the bridge.

Phil had the full re-breather on. His voice reverberated, "No bike, today?"

"Much going on?"

"You know, they don't do well when the weather warms. They turn bitey."

I could hear the growls emanating from below along with the occasional crack and snap cutting through the overall grumbling. "They sound restless."

"It's the season. The herd will thin itself out over the next few months."

I could not see his face under the mask, but I imagined Phil preferred to bury his feelings under layers. The rest of his family existed down below, leaving me unsure he could face losing them again.

"You have a second?" asked Phil.

I could not hide my desire to move away from the smell, but I nodded.

Phil led me to the edge. "You can see them today. Right there."

I looked where Phil pointed. A medium sized walker staggered a couple steps. She wore something bright red once. Her face had gone. Two smaller figures stood nearby. One stumbled and bumped into her. She lashed out and knocked it over.

"Isn't it amazing how they have stuck together through all this?" said Phil.

I don't know when irony died for everyone else, but it happened for me when I decapitated my philosophy professor. According to my semiotics professor, irony became everyone's default point of view in the nineties. I never knew if he enjoyed the twisting knife or not. He appeared at the head of a pack of zombies who used the sheer weight of numbers to break through a plate glass window at the entryway of the science building. I had duct taped broken glass to a broomstick. On the end, I had attached a sharpened tin dustpan.

This would be the first time I wielded my makeshift weapon. Professor Gantry stumbled over zombie mess and broken glass. Everyone who had not turned ran for cover.

I decided my former professor had to be worth a swipe. I aimed for his neck and swung in a wide arc. I expected my blade to stick in bone or cartilage. I learned with time I had been lucky and made it clean through. A slurp sound and his head flew across the room. A tiny black burble replaced the professor's face and the body knelt slowly. The walker behind him tripped and fell by my feet. I dropped the broomstick and ran.

"I am sorry they're like this, Phil," I said.

"Me, too."

I could wait all day for a bright side without it arriving.

***

Frida appeared around dusk. She did not knock or even call out when she opened the door. I sat at the desk and heard her footsteps; otherwise, I don't know what I would have done. Without a word, she dropped a duffel bag and came over to sit near me.

"You brought stuff," I said.

"I'm not going back to the city tonight. Figured we might as well set off early. Dr. Kahlo is an early riser."

"Kahlo? He's your father?" I asked.

She kept right on talking. "As an early riser too, Irene probably collaborated well with him." She put her feet up on the desk. She wore black jeans and heavy boots. No one's clothes fit terribly well, but you always kept an eye out for a good pair of shoes. I had seen people take them off zombies when they couldn't bring themselves to look at the rest of the corpse. "Are you squatting here now?" She raised an eyebrow.

"We don't have much of a station in these parts," I answered, "so I didn't want to impose on those guys."

"Very thoughtful of you," Frida went for her duffel. "I'll take the cot." She left the room before I decided to argue.

Surrendering to a night in a chair, I went to the back porch. I sat there five minutes before the pet carrier rattled. The black cat looked at me and I looked at him. I whistled because it made me feel casual and I ambled over to the plastic crate. Calmly, I closed and latched the door. The cat did not object until I picked up the carrier. Then, the cat made it clear it did not appreciate the tumbling and tossing. Once inside the house, I put the carrier on the desk and sat down. Frida came in and stood behind me.

"So, she's our alleged villain?" said Frida.

"Depends on who you want to believe, but I don't know how we evaluate the hypothesis. I'm not willing to let it out for the night and see what happens."

She grunted. Seeing what would happen had long ago gone out of vogue. "Your friend at the zoo might be able to put it in with other critters. It might tell us something."

"Maybe after we visit your dad,"

***

Sometime during the night, Frida woke me from my sleep in the chair and led me upstairs. She had done something with the bed covers which made them slightly less disgusting. She proved as careful as everyone to avoid any chance of children.

I awoke alone in a jumble of three or four blankets. One of them sent a flurry of dust flying as I sat up. Stumbling downstairs, I heard Frida on the front porch. I headed for my pack first and went through my morning ablutions on the back porch. The black cat glared at me as I passed by it. I offered him water.

On the front porch, I smelled coffee before I saw the cup in Frida's hand. She held it carefully. A dopey grin bloomed on her face. "A little girl brought this over from the neighbors. She said welcome to the neighborhood."

"From the Partridge family, I imagine."

Frida raised an eyebrow, and I decided I liked the expression on her. "I haven't taken a sip yet. I want the aroma to enter all my pores. I won't bathe for a week. I'll sniff my forearm every morning."

"Eau d'caffeine," I christened.

She dipped her fingertip in the cup and dabbed behind each ear. "Do you want the rest? I never did like the taste."

"I know where those fingers have been. I think I'll pass."

She rose to her feet and tossed the remaining coffee into the bushes. "You ready to go see the professor?"

"What should we do with the cat?" I asked.

"It might be interesting to see if the professor recognizes it."

I grabbed water and snacks for the trip, and we set off. After two blocks, I wanted to ditch the pet carrier. Frida told me to sit in the shade. Twenty minutes passed and she returned with a child's wagon.

In the process of reclaiming the South Wedge, the streets had been through the first stage of cleaning. People made large litter piles along one side or burned the garbage leaving blackened clumps. Our immediate predecessors rolled all the vehicles to one side, making at least one clear lane of passage. In the process, they scavenged anything useful. Glove compartments and trunks sat sprung open. Batteries looted. Assuming the Mayor received his cut, the goods wound up in the police barracks. However, His Honor's office passed the batteries on to the techies.

Three blocks with the kid's wagon and it became clear why no one had claimed it. The squeaky wheel only enhanced the aggravation of the wobbly axle.

"So, you're taking me to meet your father?" I asked.

"I'm taking you to meet Professor Kahlo. This is no social call. He won't talk to me."

"As a daughter or as a journalist?"

"Look, he's been working on all kinds of things since everything went down," said Frida. "I can't always understand what he says. You studied science in college. You'll weasel more out of him."

"Wait... Do you mean he's still doing research? How? Into what? And Irene helped him?"

"If I could convince him to tell me, then I wouldn't need you or the cat," said Frida.

"Do you really think it had something to do with Irene's death?"

Frida stopped walking and took a swig from a water bottle. "No... maybe. Does it matter?"

"I'm supposed to be investigating her murder."

Frida grunted.

"What?" I asked.

"It's the first time you called it a murder." When I did not respond, Frida offered, "Does it make you feel like a grown-up detective?"

"Not particularly."

We stopped outside Mt. Hope Cemetery.

"You ever wonder if Frederick Douglas came back?" asked Frida. "They buried him up there."

"You think he'd advocate on behalf of the undead?" I responded.

"I'd like to meet him. He lived in the time of broadsheets. He might offer useful advice."

"Finding it tough to gain attention for your paper?"

According to most people, Rochester's troubles began in Mt. Hope Cemetery. When the dead walk, they also climb out of wherever we bury them. People had not constructed crypts for this situation. Perhaps the newly risen returned stronger than they had been in life. Not my experience, but every apocalypse requires a popular explanation. I always figured the morgue had it much worse during those first few hours.

The cemetery sits next to campus, and I never saw any evidence which led straight back to graves. Maybe the zombies had been down there somewhere, but the undead never pockmarked the grounds of the cemetery with holes where they had clawed their way to the surface. This plague started not as something other than a twisted version of the rapture.

Strong Hospital filled a huge expanse across from Mt. Hope Cemetery. You wanted to avoid medical facilities in those first few days. The ER overflowed with unusual symptoms, although they became usual quickly enough. Parts of the hospital became ruins. You never really think about how explosive so many things are until you have first-hand experience.

Circling past the remains of the hospital power plant, we entered the university campus. Throughout the city, sanitation services have become hit and miss. The Mayor made it a priority and more people worked to bring water in and remove sludge and trash. The South

Wedge had central locations for dumping which went a long way toward reducing blowing trash and the general aroma.

Unfortunately, municipal staff had not approached the campus yet. It looked like fraternity parties overran the entire college and then the partiers deserted it about a year ago. Beer cans piled in windless corners. Trash hung from trees and power lines. A couple of the modern buildings looked worse for wear. Their windows had shattered, a side effect of not opening once the air conditioning ceased working.

Frida led me to one of the old science buildings, more descript than the concrete block structures. We entered through a side door and headed to the basement. The lights on, I hesitated when they flickered, but Frida proceeded down the hall. We passed a blood-splattered notice board for activities and opportunities long past.

She paused before a closed door and motioned toward it. "Aren't you going in?"

Never keen to burst in on someone, I hesitated, "Does he react well to surprises?"

"You'll be fine." Frida nudged me forward.

I remembered I needed to behave like a cop and a grown up. Then I conjured a mental image of myself over the last few years. I turned the doorknob and went in anyway. An old-style chemistry lab classroom, I halted as the entire room came into focus. Each table bore equipment in a different configuration. Next to one setup, the professor scribbled notes without looking up, alone, sort of. Body parts, probably zombies, made up pieces of whatever experiments covered four tables.

In the far corner, a whole zombie sat in a chair, chained, and gagged. A large cage beside it held the top half of another zombie. They both looked at me, but generated none of the usual whining, gurgling, and groaning. Between the lack of ventilation and the volume of rotten flesh, a palpable haze stung the back of my throat. An unpleasant odor burned my tongue as I breathed through my mouth.

Finally, the Professor glanced up, nodded in my direction, and went back to his notes. The apocalypse may have provided him with the time to do exactly what he wanted for the first time in his life.

"Hello, sir, I'm front the Rochester Police Department."

He held very still, as if processing this information. He set the pad of paper aside. "What did you say?"

"I'm from the Rochester Police Department. I hoped to ask you a few questions."

He looked at me, taking a moment to bring me into focus. His voice betrayed no passion, but his words revealed a great deal of feeling. "Is it over? Or is it all in my head?" Before I could answer, he turned his head and saw the abominations in the corner. The lab coat he wore hung loosely, but I saw him sag within it.

"Are you Professor Kahlo?"

His manner changed quickly. He settled onto a nearby stool and looked interested. "I guess I am. Who are you?"

"I am Officer Crash, sir. I used to go to this university as a science undergraduate. I stayed behind when things went bad."

"I don't remember you," said Kahlo, "but I taught graduates mostly."

I recalled his reputation as one of the shining lights who brought in enough research money to fund his own lab. "No, sir, I never studied anything with you."

"Too bad," Kahlo frowned sincerely. I would never take a class with him now. "How are things out there? We have a police department now. Without uniforms or badges?"

"We have badges." I pulled mine out.

He waved it off.

"What are you doing down here, sir?"

He looked at me as if it should be obvious, not the first person to do so. "I'm looking for a cure."

Normally, I greeted people who said similar things with a nod and backing away. Usually, they had plastic bottles gurgling away over a fire or strange powders growing mold in a pan or weird chants and prayers at the ready. For the first time, I heard those words and accepted they might not be powered by bullshit. "How is it going?"

Kahlo removed his glasses and massaged the bridge of his nose, "Slowly." He considered me. "How many hours did you put in before your studies ceased?"

"Made it to third year. I spent the first stretch after things fell apart stuck in a chemistry classroom with Professor Donaldson."

He looked at me hard, unwilling to ask the question. When I did not let him off the hook by continuing to talk, he broke the silence. "How is Frank?"

"He didn't make it." I watched the zombies for a minute, taking my first opportunity to look at one after the adrenalin rush had passed. My impression had always been of pack predators, like wolves. Alone, they appeared forlorn. "Are you all by yourself here?"

"We don't really keep regular hours anymore. People come and go as they please."

"How many have come and gone in the past week?" I asked.

"I'm not so good with time," said Kahlo. "This isn't something new, but it's probably worse with age."

No one to look after you, I thought. "Professor, when did you last eat or have a drink of water?"

He paused.

I gently took his arm. "Do you have any food or water?"

He shook free. "I am not senile! I am forgetful, but I eat when I am hungry, and I drink when I am thirsty." Kahlo headed toward the door. "Come with me."

He headed down the hall. Frida had gone somewhere out of sight. The professor opened one of the classroom doors. I stopped in the entryway, stunned. Someone had brought in boxes of C-rations and bottled water. He had coffee and chocolate, potato chips and Twinkies. He pushed past me and continued down the hall.

"Where does it all come from?" I asked.

Kahlo opened another door. He had one generator running and a spare waiting in the wings, very high-end models, vented through holes cut in the walls. "I store the gas outside."

"I need an explanation, Professor."

"I don't have one. It's the food fairy, I suppose."

I followed Kahlo back to his lab. "How long have you been down here?"

"Since the troubles." Kahlo offered me bottled water he had grabbed during his tour. He pushed an open box of Hostess cakes toward me. "Look, the incident behaved like a disease, and I thought I could help. College students surrounded me, facing neither a video game nor the cool adventure movie they had envisioned. Almost all died very quickly which made this an exponentially worse situation."

I pointed a cake at the zombies in the corner. "Is this where they came from?"

"Not exactly, we felt secure here and the problem had been in the news for a brief time."

"I remember those first news stories became hysterical quickly."

The professor shook his head. "It only happened when the plague idea caught hold. Since then, others have suggested a radiation cause or something which would cause all the dead to return, but reports supported no such things. If instantaneous and universal, then it should not be contagious. Is there any new data?"

"Locally? No."

"Good, then my suppositions remain correct. The only ones who turn are those infected prior to death. Of course, we're all affected now."

It could explain Frederick Douglas and all the others long dead in the cemetery staying put. I saw what he meant. "You're looking for a cure?"

He unwrapped his cake and took a bite. "The important thing proved to be how little I cared about leaving. I have been divorced for an awfully long time. My friends are adults. I assumed they took the necessary steps to survive. I had no expectation of a rescue.

"As the months passed, I watched people leave the building. Most made it out of sight. In the end, six of us remained. I spent the intervening time working on a solution to the problem. I had a graduate student named Hemper. He came from Germany. He kept our communications going. Others foraged for food, water, batteries, and things. I think Hemper must have been an electrical engineer. Either way, he performed miracles. Because of him, I stayed connected with other scientists working on the problem."

I raised my hand. "Which problem?"

Yet again, Kahlo looked at me as though I missed the obvious. Then, his expression changed. "Actually, it's an interesting question. Once you address the issue of day to day survival, which everyone else had to manage, then the question becomes one of identification. What transpired? Therefore, we observed and made notes. We produced a hypothesis and refined it. Understand when I say we, I mean all the locations still actively doing research."

"You've been in touch with how many places?"

"You'd be surprised. Of course, we had to take them at their word about their location. They presented legitimate work."

"How far away are they?"

"All over the globe- did you not notice the satellite dish on the roof? We don't notice things anymore."

Already far afield from my murder investigation, a little further did not matter. International news had not been a thing for a long time. "Did the plague hit everywhere as hard? Europe? Asia? Africa?"

Kahlo paused. "My information comes from people like me, people who found a bunker somewhere and proved smart enough to stay in it. With that in mind, it sounds bad everywhere."

"No one mentioned a safe zone, any place free of the things, Greenland or somewhere?"

"People mention places all the time and then rule them out as more information arises. I'm sorry." Kahlo bit his cupcake. "But we are not without hope. You're here, Mr. Police Officer, which means society is trying to return. More importantly, my colleagues and I have agreed on a hypothesis. This is a disease, probably airborne. Its effect on all living organisms studied so far is negligible. Certain creatures experience post-mortem symptoms, notably reanimation. The important fact is this is a disease and therefore we can treat or cure it."

"What about prevention?"

"Too late," said Kahlo. "With a newborn's first breath, the disease enters them. If you mean preventing the symptoms, I imagine people are trying to, aren't we? They shoot zombies, don't they? Otherwise, no one would be alive, would they?"

"You never explained about all your food? Where does it come from?" I asked.

"A little more than a year ago, we received word help might be coming."

"Who's coming?"

"I assumed the government," said Kahlo. "Word spread months before the federal government had come back online. In many ways, it never stopped functioning. A cataclysm on this scale prevented nations from engaging in state-sanctioned cross-border conflict." He drank water. "Only four of us remained when the soldiers arrived."

"You saw armed forces in actual uniforms?" I thought about the army escorts who accompanied the convoy. "When?"

"About a year ago, they behaved very well, like you," said Kahlo. "No one did anything violent inside. They cleared the yard, but not much to do by then."

"And they brought you food and water?" At about the same time, the Mayor decided to reclaim the South Wedge. Helpfully, the army had been in Rochester escorting one of the first convoys from New Jersey. They volunteered to protect the workers sent in to extend the walls.

"They also brought the generators and new laptops and Hostess." The professor held up his cupcake and took a bite. "I appreciated the coffee the most. We didn't do a responsible job of rationing in the early days."

"No one did. How could we envision this much bad for so long?" One of the zombies in the corner shuffled, bringing me back to the present. "Did you ask them why? Where they are from?"

"What do you mean?" Kahlo looked worried. I may have pushed too hard for an old survivor who had managed to dig a hole to hide in for the past few years. People grew used to their bunkers and lost their minds when they first set foot back outside. "They came from the army. They brought messages from the CDC. My research mattered to them. I contribute to a cure." He went and grabbed his laptop. "Here, I'll show you."

Kahlo told the truth. The URL's looked legitimate. We had no way to confirm who lived on the other end, but the professor had gigabytes of exchanges with the CDC and CERN and scientists scattered everywhere. Somewhere along the way, the U.S. government had taken notice. In my world, federal authority had not mattered from the day we blocked all the exits to the day I stepped outdoors and inhaled. "You said four of you lived here? What happened to them?"

The professor shuffled through old emails. "They moved out once it became apparent they should be safe."

"But you stayed?"

"I like it here," said Kahlo.

"Do you still see them? Does anyone help with your research?"

"Irene comes around. I haven't seen the other one in months." Kahlo swiveled in his seat. "And there's Donald." He pointed at the zombie in the chair.

We contemplated Donald; no longer the person named Donald. For its part, the thing rolled its head, roared mutely at the ceiling, and gave us the evil eye.

Everyone argues about the intelligence of zombies. They look at you so impassively it is difficult to ascribe any thought to them. They are as capable of low cunning as the next predator. Never underestimate them or you end up like Donald.

"What happened to him?" I could guess, but I couldn't stop from asking. The professor's zombies loomed like undead elephants in the room.

"We kept the other specimen around for our experiments. Donald became careless." Kahlo's voice softened. "The bravest man I ever met, Donald ensured we survived down here. When we needed something, he went outside. When things looked the worst, he gave everyone strength. I'm not the same kind of man. I didn't notice how people felt or what we needed to make it through the next day and then...

"He came back with a bite about two months ago. We knew what would happen and how quickly, the harsh calculus of death... He willed himself to science. He chained himself to the chair. We documented the change in him. There had been others, but he has really become our baseline and our greatest controversy."

"I don't understand," I admitted.

"Really very resilient, Donald documented verbally what transpired within his own mind far longer than anyone else before him could. This re-opened for debate exactly what happens to the bitten. If you go ahead and die, then you turn within six hours. Many people turn quicker, but it's an average.

"On the other hand, what happens when one of those creatures bites a living person? Do we observe a morphological event? Does death occur? We assumed it must, but with Donald... Clearly in distress, particularly near the end, his change happened so quickly."

"You're wondering if death is the trigger?" I asked.

"You see, don't you? If death is not, then this might be parasitic or something else--"

"Not a virus or not something which can be treated?"

We considered a world unable to become normal again. Everyone clung to such a hope. Even if it never happened, those of us who remembered could hang onto such a vision. I studied at Donald. He looked and smelled dead.

I turned back to the professor. "Are you also saying he might still be Donald over there and he can be cured?"

"Looking at him, I know it seems patently absurd."

The other thing about the dead is all their eyes look the same- lifeless, dry. "Tell me about the others. What about Irene?"

The professor ran his fingers through his hair, a gray crackle followed by a shower of dandruff. "She's a good kid. She moved out like all the rest, but she came back to help. She might have been sweet on Donald."

I looked across the room. Zombies are all biters, with or without teeth. "When did she last come here?"

The question caught the professor's attention. "Four or five days ago, she did a little work and picked up food."

"Did anything happen to her while here?"

He looked at me. I looked back.

Kahlo broke first. "Like what? She helped with slides. Her eyes are younger. I haven't had a new pair of glasses in years."

"Anything else?"

"No, no," Kahlo's expression hardened. "What's going on?"

I took a deep breath. "Irene is dead. I'm trying to find out what happened."

A series of masks contorted his face. Doubt changed to disbelief changed to curiosity changed to grief followed by anger. I thought the last one might stick, but then exhaustion won out. He tried to speak once or twice and succeeded with. "Why?"

"It's what I want to know."

"No, why are you investigating it? What makes her death so special? Why don't you investigate Donald's demise? Or any of those others I watched die right outside the window?"

"You know the answer, Professor. We know how those people died. I wouldn't be looking into Irene's death if we could say the same in her case."

"Don't condescend to me," bitterness crept into Kahlo's voice. "It might work for the masses. We don't need police investigations of how people died. Will you scrutinize those who murdered their comrades in their bunkers because food ran short? Are they also out of mind now? What are you doing about this damn plague? Are you certain it isn't the bigger crime?"

"I can't be certain about much," but Kahlo pissed me off. "But I can try for one thing today. Moreover, if I'm lucky, I can be certain about one thing tomorrow."

"I think I remember you now," Kahlo grimaced. "You sat in the back and grinned all the way through class like you had a little joke playing in your head. Life stopped being a joke and now you interfere with your betters who do the real work."

I didn't feel like any more cake. I wiped my hands on my pants. "Whether or not you accomplish anything here, the world outside your lab needs to keep turning."

Kahlo found something interesting to examine on the ceiling. "You come in here spouting about Irene's death." He tore a page from his notebook and slowly ripped it into strips. "There has been so much death. I can't let you distract me. We're closer every day."

The room had shrunk. Walls closed in and became hard to bear. I swam through a sea of information, seeking pearls. "Can you tell me why Irene might have a lab in her basement?"

I gave Kahlo pause. "She did research on her own?"

"I don't know, but someone filler her basement with laboratory equipment." I didn't feel obliged to be completely forthcoming on the state of her setup.

Kahlo gave it a thought. "Did she have everything we have here?" His arms swept the contents of the lab.

"Not the satellite hookup and minus the zombies."

"But a chemistry workplace?"

I shook my head. "Wouldn't hold a candle to what you have here."

Kahlo grabbed at possibilities. "She had ideas of her own. What did her notebooks say?"

"I didn't find anything remotely recent."

"Irene had been through everything alongside the rest of us, but she never stopped being a good scientist. There would be notebooks."

"Do you have any idea why someone would want to hurt her?" I asked.

Kahlo gave me a withering look. "Haven't you lived through the recent past? What have we been talking about here? Do people need a reason anymore?"

I thanked the professor for his time. When I left, I took my half-eaten cupcake and bottle of water with me. Once in the hallway, I closed the lab door behind me before the shudders took hold. They gradually subsided. I couldn't find Frida.

Avoiding the temptation to loot the Professor's stash, I headed for the exit. I found the wagon and pet carrier outside. Annoyed at the world in general and the professor in particular, I grabbed the carrier and hauled it down to his lab. I made a noisy entrance, startling the man and the monsters. "One last thing before I leave you to your work," I spat. "Does this cat look familiar to you?"

He looked at me calmly and then at the cat curiously. My anger encouraged compliance. I had seen it before when trapped with others during the first few weeks. Leadership is much more fluid than old how-to books might have you believe. Everyone followed whoever projected the most pissed off in the moment.

"I haven't had an animal in here in years," said Kahlo. "One of the women students rescued a puppy as I recall, but no cats."

"This belonged to Irene. People say it scratched her before she turned."

"Did anyone actually witness the sequence of events? No? I am not surprised. Only anecdotes have emerged linking cats to deaths, except where the person caught something else fatal because of the animal. Perhaps this little one has something else going on?"

I hadn't considered such. "Doctor Darwin at the zoo agrees with you. Pets are not carriers."

"Darwin? I don't remember meeting anyone by the name in all my years in Rochester."

"You might not have. Quite a few people took new names when they climbed out of whatever hole they'd sheltered in."

The professor nodded. "May I keep our little friend here? I'd like to see if your story has any basis."

"It's not my story." The thought of carrying the cat around any longer did not appeal. I wondered what type of death its claws carried. "No problem. You keep it."

I looked on the upper floors of the building before I left, hoping to find Frida. I saw furniture in broken jumbles. Previous visitors scavenged the rooms thoroughly.

Walking back to Irene's, the professor gave me plenty to think about, but it didn't have much to do with my case. I wondered why Frida had brought me to him. I finished the water and the cake before I arrived back at the house. None of the Partridges appeared outside when I passed their home. Before I hit the hay, I decided to head downtown in the morning.

Eight

“What I am hearing is you don't have a suspect and the girl might've died of natural causes.” Sarge leaned back in his chair and crossed his arms.

“I don't know if I'd describe it the same way.”

“Look, you found the coffee,” he held up his hands, “I have the whole story on the case, don't you worry, but it does not buy you a lot of time to traipse around for no good reason.” He neglected to mention the amount of time I spent traipsing would be completely his decision.

“If this is a murder, then it needs looked into,” I argued. “We can't have someone running around threatening people in the city after all the progress we've made.”

“What about this professor over at the university?” asked Sarge. “He might have helpful loot. It could be worth looking into. Who's his supplier?”

“I think it's the Feds, something to do with the convoys.”

Sarge nodded. "All right, I'll put guys on it. We'll stake out the truckers next time and see who goes for a little trek upriver. Let's say this intelligence has bought you a couple more days on the investigation."

"It works for me."

"Glad to hear it, but I am not wasting any more time on this if you don't turn up something we can use to promote our good deeds."

I understood why Sherlock spent so much time alone on the roof in recent months. I would have been better off as a patrol officer.

***

The printing presses of the *Democrat and Chronicle* remained on the first floor of their building wedged between the police station and our barracks, but they would not come back online anytime soon. I needed the active presses, wherever the news broadsheets originated. Since they tended to be critical of the Mayor, they kept a low profile. I suspected His Honor knew their location.

I had never looked for them. My friend, Diocletian, worked among the techies at the library. He pointed me toward the broadsheet's not-so-hidden location, and I only had to listen to an hour of economic theory.

I headed to Culver Street on my bike. An old sign lying on the ground indicated the building had housed a commercial printer. Across the street, the remains of a gym crumbled. At one time, large plate glass windows allowed passersby to admire the physiques within. Those windows had presented a buffet under glass to any passing zombie.

I opened the door to the printer and a little bell tinkled. I waited in the entryway for a moment until a "Hello!" greeted me. I called out and headed down the hall. A young man intercepted me. He had carefully closed the door behind him after he appeared. He held a rag, wiping ink off his hands. "How can I help you?"

"I'm looking for the broadsheet editorial offices. I understand they're here?"

"I'm afraid somebody told you wrong." He turned to go back to his work.

"You misunderstand me. I've been working with one of the reporters. I need to see her."

"I still can't help you." He tried again to leave.

"You still seem to misunderstand. I'm not asking. I'm coming in." He blocked my way.

"Let's not do this," I said. When he didn't budge, I kicked him in the nuts. I strolled past him. "I said I didn't want to do it." Behind the door, I found another hallway. This one led to a variety of doors. The first opened on a bathroom which smelled of death and disinfectant and asparagus. The most in demand person in the world had to be a plumber.

After, I proceeded a little slower opening the next door, which turned out to be an empty supply closet. Finally, a large room was set up for screen-printing. Its former occupant stayed out front lowering his voice before he staggered into my hallway. I glared at him, and he paused. "Well?" I asked. He leaned against the wall and gestured with two fingers toward the door at the other end.

As I pushed, another bell jingled. By the time I crossed the threshold, I faced ten unhappy people sitting behind desks and pointing various unpleasant objects at me. I held very still until I made it clear nobody needed to shoot, stab, or otherwise harm me. I tried my most disarming smile. I did. I had never tried one before. I stopped trying it when my lips felt more like a maniacal grin. "Hi," I attempted. No one responded. "I'm looking for a friend who works here." The room relaxed. "This is the broadsheet, right?"

An older man came out from behind a desk. "Why don't you tell me who it is you expected to find here?" The denizens returned to their previous activities, which involved writing and drawing.

"She called herself Frida. She's about five three and thin. She has brunette hair." No light bulbs went off. "She said she worked here. I met her running around in the South Wedge. She's looking into the cause of the plague, I think."

This stranger owned a great poker face. "I might know her. What do you want with her, officer?"

"Come on, it can't be so obvious already. We barely have a city and you're telling me it's already easy to pick out the cops?"

A smile briefly cracked his face, but he fixed it quickly. "The law always looks and acts like the law." He went back and sat down. From his perch, he considered me carefully, reached a decision, and motioned me over, "What would your name be, son?"

"Crash- I met Frida while looking into the death of her friend, Irene."

"And you think this Frida might be involved?" asked the editor.

"I'd be lying if I said she didn't know more than she told me, but no, I'm not looking to implicate her. She's been a help so far and right now I could use more help."

"What's so important about another death?" He sounded like a reporter when he asked.

"It might have been murder," I could care less about any quotes appearing in the broadsheet. How many people read the thing? Maybe if they included sports scores. That would require sports to occur.

"Among all the other ongoing horrors, what difference does it make?" asked the editor.

My body felt tired of justifying my job to everyone I met, especially when I considered it only a job, I wanted to know what happened to Irene because it took my mind away from what I had seen, and gave me a moment to focus elsewhere. Unfortunately, the people of the city needed a better reason to cooperate with me. "At any point, wouldn't you like us to worry about murders again?"

The editor shrugged. "You do realize the worst murder rates in the country never came close to one percent? Deaths from heart disease and cancer far exceeded it. Now we face this new insanity. If you are asking me how I think we ought to utilize our limited resources, then I might suggest healthcare. Don't forget we had a police force six months before the first clinic opened. Thank you, Mr. Mayor."

"But I'm not a doctor."

"No time like the present to learn." He gave me another long, appraising look, and his expression softened. "You don't need me to bust your balls. People used to say things like 'I'm only doing my job' and then the rest of us would go about our labors."

It took me a minute of patience to realize he performed for an audience. The room's occupants had stopped their work. Our Goofus and Gallant show enraptured them. I had the short end of the stick and wanted out. "Can you help me find Frida or not? I'm only trying to do my job." I did not appreciate the snickers after those words passed my lips.

He smiled benevolently, pissing me off further. "She usually comes in on Thursdays. If you wait in front tomorrow, then you'll see her."

"One last thing, sir."

"What?"

"What's your name?"

His smile grew even bigger. "Ben, Ben Franklin. I'd spell it for you, but you don't seem to carry a notebook."

I stopped walking away because my anger took root. "You are a condescending prick. Everybody really is trying to survive. I don't remember seeing you out there staffing the fences, cleaning the streets, or emptying bedpans in your precious clinic. Who are you to act so goddamn special?"

The biggest person in the room stepped in my path.

The old man didn't blink, "Nobody, Officer, other than the person who made you think about the clinic."

I stormed out of the building, jingling bells all the way.

***

I regret my choices over the next few hours, but I let Ben Franklin push my buttons. The next morning, I stood across the street from the printer. I hid in the former gym, well covered by shadows and boredom. Sarge waited up the street with police officers. I held a whistle in one hand and sweat in the other. Too late, it dawned on me I did not approve of what we had planned. It's a fine line bearing the words "just doing my job" and "just following orders" and they can move far afield from where you ought to be.

I recognized faces from the previous day as they came and went. Good old Ben showed up. I waited. The sun found the middle of the sky and still I waited. My water ran out and I moved deeper into the shade.

A mile distant, the undead pen wafted the special scent of zombie everywhere. The pall hung over everything, but not so heavily in my hiding place. When we all lived in close quarters, the funk blossomed so horribly our eyes burned if we moved into proximity to another human being, but we knew better than to complain since our own mess floated equally palpably. Even with everything in the air, we could smell a zombie at twenty paces. It's not far, but it's not bad for the human nose. It kept the surviving animals alive.

Frida entered my peripheral vision. While waiting for her, I reconsidered the original plan of busting the whole broadsheet clan. I ran across the street and thankfully, she stopped in her tracks when she saw me. "I've been looking all over for you," I said.

"Sounds a lot like lying in wait," Frida said. "Well, you found me."

"Professor Kahlo is not your father." I should have led with something else.

"No flies on you, Sherlock."

I had to stop myself from telling her Sherlock waited back at the station. "Why did you take me to see him?"

"I thought he might help with your investigation. We're doing this for my friend, Irene, remember? I wouldn't mind seeing a little justice done." She wore a loose top and even looser jeans, cinched with a belt. She scratched her bare arm, waiting for me to produce more words.

"I don't think so. You wanted me to find out about the professor." Then I remembered Sarge. He saw me standing in the middle of the road because he barreled toward us at the head of a passel of cops.

"What the fuck, Crash?" Frida kicked me in the shin and ran in the opposite direction.

Sarge slowed to a steady walk. No one passed him, so he arrived first, "Always a credit to the uniform, son. I saw the young lady leave you in her dust."

"She's a lot tougher than you'd think, sir."

"They all are." Sarge examined the building before us. "Am I looking at the door?"

I repeated my earlier description of the interior.

"And you figure it's payday?"

"Only reason I can see for everybody showing up; it's not like they punch a clock."

"What do you suppose they are paid with?" asked Sarge.

"I have no idea."

"And there's maybe ten or twenty inside?" After I nodded, he looked over the pack of human brutality arrayed behind him. He had selected his usual group of hardcore misfits. "We have this. Why don't you go chase down the young hellcat and see what kind of other useful information you can detect?"

***

I had no clever ideas for finding Frida. The printer contained my best hope for leads and I had well and truly burned my bridge. MLK Park lay on my way back to the station, so I veered off toward there. Tragedy looked nowhere in sight, but he might have hidden in a shady nook or cranny. Gathered teens huddled together, and a loner read a book. I found a perch and rested my legs.

A poke in the ribs startled me awake, as I must have dozed off. A burst of bad breath enveloped my head. "It's a tragedy," said he and then leaned away.

"Hey," I groaned and licked my teeth. "I didn't see you earlier. Is everything all right?"

MLK Park looks like something Escher would design if he felt particularly public spirited. Concrete steps and plateaus sprout metal scaffolding, all of which have no destination. Outdoor concerts used to happen there. Tragedy pointed to one of the myriad hiding places. "It's a tragedy."

"I'd have to agree with you." Conversations with Tragedy had their own rhythm, which I found comforting. Substitute something appropriate whenever he spoke and the two of you could while away an afternoon.

He grabbed my elbow and pointed again. "It's a tragedy."

Of course, he rarely acted adamant. "I suppose I can take a look." I rose to my feet, but I stopped there.

Frida's head popped up. She turned and blinked like a prairie dog. Then her head disappeared again with a little eek. With hands on hips, I waited. The next time, she stood all the way. "I suppose you're going to wait all day if I don't come out." She climbed onto a riser a little higher than my position. "I know you're good at staking out."

"Patience is a requirement for the force."

Frida jumped from platform to platform until she stood beside me. "Are you going to keep chasing me until I answer your questions?" She sat beside Tragedy.

"What's going on is all I want to know." I sat on the other side of Tragedy.

He looked uncomfortable, caught between the two of us.

"You sure you want to lead with a big question? Do you mean it in the existential sense?"

"You know what I mean," I said.

"Fine, we'll play it your way," said Frida. "I thought the Professor would have been walking the path of knowledge. Didn't the two of you have a good talk?"

"I learned a lot. You're right, but he didn't tell me much about Irene."

"Did you see his lab?" asked Frida.

"All right, maybe Donald gummed her."

"It's a tragedy," sputtered out between us.

Frida stayed quiet.

I soldiered on, "Fine, first things first. What's your real name?"

"Are we doing real names now, Officer 'Crash'?"

"All right, fine. What do people call you these days?"

"You can call me Frida."

I sulked and searched for another line of inquiry. "Did you already know about all this stuff the Professor is up to?"

"Yea," she nodded.

"Then why haven't you written anything about it?"

She glared at me. "I have."

Fed up with being the buffer, Tragedy clambered to his feet and stalked away, shaking his head.

"What do you expect to come out of this?" I asked. "Nobody's going to be worked up about one scientist in a basement on the outskirts of town."

"It's not the issue," said Frida. "Where does he obtain the food? Who is keeping him alive? He's involved in something big."

"I don't think he knows any more than we do," I saw so many dead ends. "I'm not at all convinced his experiments are accomplishing anything either."

"What about Irene?" Frida surrendered to my hopelessness. "Fine, I'll go back to the broadsheet and write something up. Maybe somebody will read it who can accomplish something. At least I'm trying..."

I held up my hand to ebb the tide of her indignation. "You might think about staying away from there today."

You could see the wheels turning in Frida's head as she processed my statement. "You might not have been staking me out personally? Could this be about the broadsheet?" Like a faux fortuneteller spinning out the truth by reading my expression after each word, she continued, "Other cops raided the office. No one there will ever trust me again."

"Sarge won't screw it up for you," I may not have believed it myself.

"Forgive me if I'm not willing to trust my reputation to the discretion of a bunch of Neanderthals and bullies who barely have enough brains between them to protect themselves, let alone a whole city. None of you has any idea what's been going on or even what matters. Hell, none of you cares. And now you've taken away the one platform I had."

"Come on, they'll take you back," I insisted.

"You're an idiot." Frida moved away. "I thought you had enough brains to accomplish something, but no."

I watched her go. Her anger left a visible wake. Looking around, I saw we had been the center of attention for a time. People took their entertainment where they could find it. We really needed to have television back so people could go back to ignoring one another.

***

Seeing how the police force had only recently identified their second active detective , I had limited choice in the peers I could consult. I found Sherlock in the station cafeteria, a first for me. "I didn't realize you ever deigned to eat indoors."

Sherlock shrugged. "There's a limit to how tolerant the pigeons can be and today they reached it. Besides, Gladys has always been sweet on me, and the occasional visit encourages her to keep me in her thoughts." He waved a chocolate chip cookie at one of the lunch women, who proceeded to turn bright pink.

"I haven't seen chocolate chips in forever."

Sherlock took a big bite, chewed slowly, and swallowed dramatically. "It helps if you're more of a people person."

He jerked my chain, but I couldn't decide how hard it would be. He had crazy long hair, an invitation for a lice outbreak, even though he tied it in a clean ponytail, looking like a short salt and pepper mane. For spring, he skin glowed bronze. The cracks on his face cut deep and probably hid scars. Other than the hair, Sherlock's eyes always stoned me- steel gray and still shining. Many fires had gone out in many eyes, and it helped to see somebody continuing to pay attention. "Why'd you stop being a detective?"

"Who says I stopped?" Sherlock finished his cookie and brushed his hands off.

"I didn't know," I mumbled. "Are you working on something?"

"Son," said Sherlock, "you may find this hard to believe, but I've been working on the same case for almost a year now."

"On the roof?"

Sherlock smiled. "Let's say I ran into a few roadblocks."

Leaning back in my chair, I wondered what could have stopped Sherlock. I guessed the Mayor. "If you're still a functioning cop, can I run what I'm working on by you?"

He glanced at his bare left wrist. "It's only a hair past a freckle. Sure, why not?"

I told him everything: Irene, Frida, Darwin, Kahlo-- my profusion of screw ups and the couple of things which made me feel proud. I didn't see a reason to hold anything back. He listened intently, hands folded, and eyes pointed at me. When I finished, he sighed and then I sighed.

Sherlock rapped the table twice. "You have a lot going on there, Crash." Before this moment, I would not have bet he knew my name.

"You have a lot of dross to separate from a little wheat if you want to solve your murder. The thing is, you don't act interested in solving the murder or else you wouldn't be running around worrying about the big picture. Murders are small picture events. Somebody does a dreadful thing to somebody else, and the story should be simple. You need to decide whether you're a little picture or a big picture guy."

"Which should I be?" I asked.

"Uh-uh, this doesn't work that way. You need to figure it out for yourself." He noticed the dismayed look on my face. "You err on the side of believing people. Remember about the big picture/little picture dichotomy- people will lie all day long, but usually not about the big picture. They don't think it matters or they aren't lying as much as they're plain wrong. It's a little easier to forgive them, but stupidity rarely serves as an excuse when bad shit happens."

He triggered something which had bothered me all day. "How did you- I mean, do you deal with everybody asking how a murder matters considering how much bad shit has gone down? Do you ever think it doesn't matter?"

"All the time, but there's an awful lot of people out there who don't give a damn about anything, or only care about the wrong things. It's always been this way and it always will. Somewhere along the line, you need to decide what matters to you.

"You're only going to last so long if you decide this is only a job, which I'll admit is one thing which has changed since the zeds popped up. Nobody needs to do anything because it's his or her job. There's always another task we need to do. We have a very fluid society right now. There's nothing saying the Mayor has to stay the Mayor or anyone else has to be what they are."

I wanted to believe freedom of speech still mattered, though not something to count on. I looked around the empty lunchroom, not happy with the attention the two lunch ladies directed our way. "I don't know anybody wants his job. He's done a lot for the city."

Sherlock smiled. "Nice to know you carry a copy of the town hymnal. Remember, you're going to have to think for yourself if you want to be any good as a detective."

Finally, my first promising idea sprouted.

Nine

I had been interested in science once upon a time. No reason I could not engage in a little observation and study of my own. For the afternoon, I dragged a lawn chair out of the barracks and rode over to Phil's post. One thing we had a lot of in the barracks had to be lawn chairs, the folding kind, and the molded plastic type. I found a folding one with a cup holder and straps so I could carry it on my back.

Phil acted a little surprised when I parked my bike and set up the chair near the edge where I had a clear view of the cage below. I shared out water and snacks. Unused to visitors, Phil adjusted. He did not even complain when I lit up the bucket-size citronella candle. Soon enough, we both had our facemasks off, enjoying a lovely day at the zoo.

I have no idea how long most folks spend studying zombies, nothing but observing them. I don't know if people who live in the jungle can ever settle down and enjoy a tiger exhibit, so I understand if a person has never chosen this particular recreation. The hours passed well enough. I always enjoyed the zoo, and I took this as an opportunity to engage in behavioral biology. For his part, Phil appreciated the company.

I asked him to point out his wife once again. Mostly sure I recognized her, I wanted to be certain. It was the warmest part of the day, though not as hot as mid-summer.

Taking the heat into account, the zombies moved terribly slowly. If I had to describe their attitude, I would say sluggish and grumpy. They spread out as wide as possible. Those with working limbs carried their arms out from their bodies and snapped at anything bumping into them. Zeds lost their fingertips this way. They had no visible problem devouring the pieces they bit off one another. However, they did not go after one another directly.

"Phil, have you ever told me how you lost your wife?"

He gave me a look as if deciding whether to insult me before he grunted softly. "I don't mind telling it again; haven't told it in a while." Phil ate the "corn" bread I brought with me. "I worked at the Penfield Wegman's for years. We did well enough to have a little house in Brighton. I'd seen all the news reports, but it seemed alien like it wouldn't come here, more like a city problem. Moreover, they were managing it.

"Then, things changed. Television broadcasts became worse amazingly fast, with so many sightings out in the county. It happened so quickly. I'd had the day before off and we went to Seabreeze, like every other day at the park. I didn't even think much about the highway spur into downtown being closed when we passed it. I felt exhausted at the end of it. We didn't watch TV when we made it home, so I missed how badly the world changed. The tipping point happened so fast.

"The next morning, I dragged my sunburned ass to work. The traffic seemed lighter, but it could be my memory playing tricks. There must have been heavy traffic somewhere because I heard later about what happened to the folks who tried to head to Canada. About ten in the morning, people came in the store and shoplifted. They stopped paying. The cashiers left. Everyone went home to their families, talking on their phones. I left, but I made it home too late.

"I don't know what happened to Julie for sure, but I imagine she went outside in the yard or tried to help someone and one of those bit her. She probably went back in and tried to clean up, but already it was too late. Then she bit Joey. I came home with a carload of supplies, but I couldn't leave my family. I locked them both in Joey's room. I made a couple more runs to the loading docks at the store and lived off the supplies until the Mayor came along."

I let us watch the shifting undead for a bit. "If I understand you correctly, you never saw them turn. You came home to a couple of zombies in the parlor."

A little anger passed his face. It's hard to remember everybody's triggers. For Phil, he hated having passers-by call out to his loved ones. He spoke through thin lips. "Actually, they paced in the kitchen. We didn't have a parlor." He mouth-breathed a moment before continuing. "No, I never saw them turn. I never spoke to them again."

I avoided pointing out to him he could still speak all he wanted to them, but the tough part would be receiving more than a growl in response. "I can't imagine staying in your house."

We watched the unhurried masses spread out below us. As the sun shone brighter, they shuffled out of sight into the shade underneath us. It's remarkable how they dispersed, not encroaching on each other's space. Reptilian behaviors came to mind as the undead rotated toward the sun, like lizards basking on rocks.

I identified groups of two or more who stayed together. At least, when they became separated, they picked up their pace in order to close the distance. I imagined they squealed with distress at those times, but I heard no such thing. The more I watched, the more I humanized everything I saw. I knew it would be a mistake with zoo animals, but these had been human once.

"Can I ask you something, Phil?"

He eyed me warily and nodded.

"I don't mean to upset you and all I'm asking for is your opinion, but do you think they're dead?"

A million thoughts expressed themselves in a full range of facial expressions and tics. "I hope not." He became interested in his hands. I had to strain to hear the next few words. "I watched what happened to them over our time in the house. At first, I gave them food, but they'd only eat raw meat. It scared me the first time I saw my son crack a bone and suck the marrow out. I fed them even after the meat turned because it didn't matter. I know people can't live off raw meat. I know it for a fact."

***

I left the chairs with Phil. Thinking I needed to talk with Doc Darwin again, I headed back to the station house with the intention of finishing out my day there. The zoo required enough of a trek to wait until morning. Besides, I wanted to think about the zombies and formulate questions. Unfortunately, I would not have the time.

As I settled in behind my desk, a runner barged onto the floor looking for Sarge. Within moments, Sarge ordered everyone available to the Mayor's office. The maelstrom of activity captured me. Weapons central handed out the large guns. We moved like a stampede as Sarge ran alongside, exhorting us to move faster. Not everyone maintained the pace and we dropped dramatically in numbers by the time we arrived at High Falls.

Sarge pulled up beside me and turned to the few remaining troops before we turned down the Mayor's street. Stragglers moseyed up to rejoin us as he spoke. "All right, something bad has gone down here and they need support. Specifically, zombie activity, but you need to keep in mind we have living people inside. Do not kill any civilians today. Let's make good choices."

He turned and we marched around the corner. The usual guard detail in front of the Mayor's place looked nowhere in sight. A small crowd of people huddled at the far end of the lane, as if they had evacuated the building after hearing a fire alarm. Sarge sent two men over to learn what they could from the bystanders. Then he gathered a team around the same entrance he and I had used just days previous.

The bystanders shared little useful intelligence. Guards charged through the main room inside and ordered everyone out. The civilians assumed zombies, but no one knew where they came from.

The Mayor did not stand outside with us, so he presumably remained inside.

Sarge picked me to go in with him for reconnaissance. No one met us when we crossed the entryway. The abattoir smell hit us right away. The main room looked a mess, but a sudden evacuation could have caused the chaos. The handfuls of zombies wandering around acted more interested in finishing their meals than trashing their surroundings. People crowded the outside balcony. Most faces watched the zeds intently through the plate glass windows.

"Why didn't they shoot the zombies?" I asked.

"Don't you remember checking your gun at the door, the guards acting more worried about the living than these others?" Sarge casually leaned against a pillar. "I count six. Want to take care of this?"

"What if there are more in another room?"

"Fine, bring reinforcements." He waited while I summoned enough for a strike force. More straggling cops had shown up while we reconnoitered inside. I pointed at ten or so to follow me. When we re-entered, Sarge had finished off the six zombies with the help of the more public-spirited citizens from the balcony. He split our people into teams to scour the building, but Sarge hung onto me.

We went out to the back porch and made our way through the crowd, receiving pats on the back and dispensing warnings about returning to the building before officers completed a thorough search. Sarge found the Mayor in one corner. His bodyguards had carved out a perimeter, but people pushed against it. Being a close satellite inferred both a degree of importance as well as a sense of safety. Neither appeared true.

I spotted Sharon yards away and deserted Sarge, who made a beeline for His Honor. Sharon had a perimeter also, but it operated on the sheer force of her personality, which expressed itself in dark clouds and a menacing scowl. I took my chances. "Bad day at City Hall?" I offered.

"Bite me," Sharon retorted, daring me to make a zombie pun.

I set my face to its most professional look. "Can you tell me what happened?"

Sharon looked like she might not, but then relented. "Our stupid coffee klatch. Look, if you work here, there are benefits. Some people are way into java. We let them in the storeroom where they could see what they could find. We have beans back there and you never know what you might uncover. They must have dug up something they shouldn't have. They had their little weekly thing in one of the meeting spaces and the next any of us know, we're facing a zombie invasion."

"Can you tell me which room?" Soon as I had the information, I raced back inside, but I arrived too late. Cantrell and Buckner had gone down as soon as they opened the conference room where the klatch met. The coffee zeds filed into the hall. The closest one swayed with each step, dangling a useless left arm. A missing chunk in its cheek gave a lovely view of its back teeth. Otherwise, his clothes had stayed remarkably clean. The disconnect in fresh zombies' appearances throws me, making it a little tougher to react violently. Any hesitation costs lives.

Fortunately, my hand reacted more intelligently than my brain. I took out the first three which slowed the ones behind them while I yelled for backup. No support appeared quickly enough so I filled the hall with debris, knocking over cabinets, and tossing around light furniture. With the time I bought, I screamed until more officers appeared. I sent Einstein out for the flamethrower. He had built the weapon a while back, but none of us entirely trusted his engineering, so we kept it outdoors unless we really needed it.

Fortunately, Sarge viewed the flamethrower as a good luck charm, so we hauled the monstrosity everywhere. For the next five minutes, we stood around throwing wastebaskets at the zombies, obstructing their progress. Nowadays, these battles become strange fights. You don't waste bullets while continuous yelling riles the damn things up, so we held a quiet skirmish. Finally, Einstein set up and flamed the hallway. He would let it rip for three seconds and then we would wait a minute. We moved along the hall five feet and repeated. Pretty soon, makeshift city hall became zombie free again.

I did not bother trailing Einstein through the halls. I bailed at the conference room. One of the zeds squirmed on the floor, so I shoved a knife into the back of its head. Then I checked out the scene. The klatch had scattered cups across the table. Apparently, once they went undead, they lost their taste for coffee. The one thing you can count on is finding a "World's Greatest..." coffee mug in any gathering. So many cups had shattered but not that one.

The coffee maker stayed intact too, which would please the survivors. Everyone appreciated finding functioning appliances, especially once we had electricity. I stared at the machine, recognizing something.... The coffee bags looked familiar; the Partridges had turned these over. They must have come from the South Wedge stash. I gathered up as much of the remains of the bag as I could and put them back in a small open bag. Then I took the dirty filter out of the machine and wrapped it in a towel. All of it found a home in my pockets.

***

Later, Sarge laughed me out of his office when I asked if we had any way to run a check for poison. Sherlock proved a little more helpful when he suggested I find a loathsome creature and feed it to them. I headed to the zoo for my overdue visit.

Dr. Darwin presided over a burial in the old rhino enclosure. I waited while she said a few words. A family I did not recognize walked past on their way home. Darwin came over, "It's still tough to lose a pet. We do what we can."

"What kind?"

"A parrot, God knows how it made it through all the bad years, but now it's time had come."

She walked and I followed. "I have a strange request, all things considered." I gave her credit for not throwing me out on my ear, but she could not help me. I provided no details. She housed nothing at the zoo which she would make available for a suicide mission. I abandoned my objective. "Can I ask about something else entirely?" I ventured as we approached the water tanks. "Do you think the zombies can be studied like other animals? Do they have behaviors we can observe, catalogue, and understand?"

"Of course." I had known Doctor Darwin for a long time. Back at the university, I spent a semester on biology, and she taught the class as an adjunct professor. Collegiate politics had led to a shakeup in the bio program. I wondered how it looked in the rear-view mirror. "They create chaos. They don't act chaotically. They have needs and methods for fulfilling those needs."

"Do you think they still have human needs?"

The question gave her pause. I could see her slip back in time. "They clearly eat, though I suppose we could debate the purpose of it since they seem capable of going prolonged periods without consuming anything. I don't know where they come down on shelter. Procreation happens through biting, so I suppose it qualifies, but it's not sex or anything we would call reproduction."

"Do they care for one another?"

She raised an eyebrow.

I continued, "They might maintain attachments after the change. I watched this mother and son, and they stayed together."

Darwin shrugged, "Interesting, what made you spend time watching zombies?"

I ignored the question. "I've been thinking about what it means."

"Hell, I don't know." Darwin turned away. "You're going down a path you don't want to. You should not identify with those things. I doubt it leads anywhere which doesn't make this life harder."

I reached out to her.

Darwin turned suddenly and dodged my hand. "A lot of people have done a lot of things that are already really hard to live with and your theory is not going to make any of it easier."

"What if it means there could be a cure?"

"A cure for what exactly, Crash? Are you going to turn those creatures back into regular people? How would it work exactly? The undead have necrosis and wounds, and god knows what else. Stopping them from being zombies means they're corpses. If you tell people to sympathize with them, then how does your cure do any good?"

"What about the ones who aren't so far gone?"

"You mean the living?" Darwin glared at me. "Look at our lives. Does your cure mean I wake up tomorrow and have my husband back? Will my daughter go to school like a normal child? Will we ever return to normal?"

"Bad idea," I mumbled. I waited for Darwin's anger to abate. "I don't suppose I could ask about one more something else entirely." I mentioned the poisoned coffee. When I asked again for an unwanted animal as a test subject, Darwin tossed me off the premises.

On the bike ride back to the station, I realized I knew one cat no one would miss.

***

Rochester used to have a bridge over I490 right by the police station, but it collapsed during the worst of times. Nowadays, the rubble lies as another feature of the zombie pits. On a muggy day when the pit residents are lackluster, spectators hang out by the fences which prevent accidental falling into the bad place and listen to the moaning under the big rocks.

I fear fate the most- a purgatory on Earth with a flicker of your humanity still burning. Can I believe in a cure? Does it matter? Would I prefer the bullet? Is this why the undead are chasing us?

After making a stop in the evidence closet at the station, I passed across Phil's bridge with as little ceremony as possible. Our prior bonding experience did not mean we had to say more than two words this time. I found Kahlo's building without any trouble. Even though only a couple of days had passed, I expected the campus to be active again and not the windswept disaster which persisted.

Sometimes smells, other times, the way the light hit the sidewalk overcame me. I would slip back in time. The sudden realization of how lost I am, like another punishing trip through the bad years, all condensed into seconds. I stood stunned until I returned comfortably to the present and finished my shaking.

The locked door at Professor Kahlo's building immediately threw a wrench in my plans. I wandered around the perimeter until I identified his lab through the basement windows. Crouching, I peered through the warped glass and decided he hid inside somewhere. I tapped and waited. No one in their right mind would wander out to investigate a strange noise, but I posited the professor did not qualify as in his right mind. Fortunately, for both of us, he knew a third path to communication.

His voice sounded through a different window. "Who?"

"Officer Crash, Professor. I hoped to speak with you."

I swear his sigh carried across the campus. "Fine, meet me at the side door."

"Which one?" but no response sounded. I had a fifty/fifty chance of this turning into a comedy routine with both of us running back and forth, but I proved lucky and met him at the right door on our first try. He grunted a greeting and turned on his heels leaving me to dive through the opening quickly as the door slammed closed again. Somebody made sure the hinges stayed in working order. I followed

Kahlo to his favorite room. Donald looked a little more glassy-eyed if possible. A Twinkies box sat opened as today's treat.

The professor did not offer me one. "What can I do for you, Officer?" he asked.

The cat cage sat where I had left it. Someone had refilled the bowl of water and added a mangled Twinkie. "I wondered how attached you've grown to the cat. I want to use it for an experiment..."

He glanced at the animal and his lips turned down. "It might be useful as a ratter, but I haven't wanted to let it out since I don't know what it might do to Donald." He reached over and jiggled the mangled pastry inside of the cage. The cat purred. "Tell me about your experiment."

Once I shared my intentions, he seemed blasé about the whole thing. I had counted on his acceptance of animal experimentation. Unfortunately, we did not have any cat chow. I mixed up a mush of Twinkie and coffee grounds with a little hamburger and a little milk. This went into a clean cereal bowl. We placed it inside the cage and waited. We could be offering the cat any number of things which might kill it. I might never know if specifically the coffee did.

We waited a while. The Professor ate very slowly without offering me anything, so I went to his supply room and retrieved my own box of donuts and a six-pack of bottled water. We sat belligerently eating at one another, looking slowly greener around the gills, and ingesting the seeds of massive pimple outbreaks.

I cracked first. "Seen your daughter lately?" I doubted Frida and he had ever been daughter and father, but I needed to make conversation.

He glared at me. His voice went soft. "My child, is she still out there?"

A million possibilities ran through my head. "I haven't seen her recently, but she's out there somewhere."

"Forgive me, Officer, but I assumed she had been put down by now."

"Frida?"

He put down his Twinkie. "I think you're making fun of my name... or maybe not. My daughter was Irene."

Then the questions tumbled out in my head as if an old closet had finally given way and I wondered how long the doubts had germinated. Instead of asking though, I said "Shit" and tossed my donut on the table where it splattered like zombie brains. After a minute of staring at my mess, I said, "I'm sorry. I didn't realize. Why didn't you say something?"

"I thought you knew. I thought you came to me because of this."

"Nope- apparently, I don't know anything, not a single damn thing. Then who is Frida?"

"Frida Kahlo, the painter?" asked Kahlo the scientist.

"I know of her, but another one runs around the city and talks about you and..."

"What does she look like?"

"Black hair, and she looks a little like the original, but smaller. Actually, I don't know how big Frida Kahlo was, so I can't say, but not big."

The Professor nodded, "The reporter."

"So, you know her?"

"She showed up here and asked questions. I'm not particularly good with timing, especially since Irene moved out, so I can't tell you exactly when. Let's say a couple of months ago. Really, I appreciated the company."

"But you haven't seen her lately?"

"Not since you first appeared," said Kahlo.

"And it didn't seem odd to you the two of you shared a surname?"

"But we didn't. She gave me a different name. She went by Ida Wells."

"Who? It sounds made up." I eyed his desktop.

"No. You may not touch the computer."

I could wait for another day. "What did Ida or Frida ask about?"

"She and Irene had been friends," said Kahlo, "and Irene put her onto me. She already knew the basics of my research as well as how we had survived. She seemed more interested in the outside world than in me."

"The outside world?"

"The computer you've drooled over," said Kahlo, "it's a Frankenstein's monster of a thing. We had a building full of IT equipment when we first locked ourselves in, but we slowly cannibalized them all and this pile of rubbish is what's left. Donald did his best, I know. You'd think the government boys would leave a laptop among all the junk food."

"Did you let Ida touch it?"

"Of course not," said Kahlo, "With Donald out of sorts, I can't take the chance."

I looked at Donald across the room, head lolled, and emitting dry rasps. "Yea, I can understand." I took a moment to soften my voice. "Can you tell me what happened to Irene?"

Even his eyes seemed to droop. "I don't know. I honestly don't know. We had never been close. Her mother remarried when Irene was quite young, and I was useless as a father. At least I felt that way. It's probably true. Irene reached out to me at about the age of twelve. I've always been grateful her mother let it happen.

"We would talk every couple of days and then nothing for months. I understood my role. She never told me anything earth shattering. Perhaps she thought so, but nothing seemed important enough to do more than listen. When it came time for college, she applied here. I thought how great, and then she took my class. I encouraged her because she had smarts. Her mother even invited me to a couple family dinners. Nice and weird and then the world went to shit."

"Life interrupted," I commented.

"I wouldn't call this life," he pointed at Donald before continuing. "And Irene became trapped here in the lab suddenly. She chose here. She didn't go to her parents." The professor crumpled up his wrappers and tossed them in a trash can.

I had seen no other building without a scattering of trash in every hall. We still made garbage, but trash dumps came and went where convenience dictated. We built midden piles for future anthropologists. His unseen support magically cleaned up after the good professor. "Of course, it's as likely her appearance occurred coincidentally since she ended up trapped here. I flatter myself. She did leave as soon as she could escape safely."

"How long ago did she move out?"

"Once we confirmed outside help. First, though, Donald had his accident, so unnecessarily. He went out one day. He said he slipped but then he showed us the bite. Nothing more to it. We set him up there, hoping to help, but it became apparent he would not recover. We restrained him." Kahlo gestured toward the zombie. "Irene's heart broke. A month later, help arrived. She took longer and longer trips away. But she always came back."

"She's not coming back this time, Professor."

Kahlo walked to the windows and cleaned his glasses on his lab coat. "They tell me they're going to bring an optometrist next time. I struggle to see with these."

"Who tells you and how?" I asked, but he ignored me. Some questions remained off limits. "Professor, what happened the last time you saw Irene?"

"She assembled slides. I asked about the outdoors. She told me a little about this Mayor of yours. She mentioned new neighbors, a singing group, she said. She spent a little time with Donald. Nothing else, nothing unusual."

I eyed Donald. He did not look like a threat anymore. "Could he have bitten her? What about something on one of the slides?"

"Officer, have you ever seen an undead bite someone?" asked Kahlo.

"Of course."

"The wound appears remarkably quickly. The smell is unmistakable. I would have noticed."

I had my doubts, but he sounded right as far as I recalled. "What do you think happened?"

His eyes showed the weight of years. "She's dead. It's what happened. The rest is useless errata. What difference does any of it make? Besides, how can you know the truth of it ever? Too much like claiming you can know the truth of someone else's experience."

"What about closure?" I asked.

"Words, son, a word people bandy about to restrain other people's feelings," Kahlo smiled at me for the first time. "You're young and you need to do this, so figure out what you can. For me, I have become comfortable knowing questions exist which I will never answer. What's one more? I know enough for today."

I thanked him and headed for the exit.

Kahlo stopped me. "Officer, I think you might have a clue here, however."

We both looked at the dead cat in the carrier. He made me take the corpse with me.

Ten

I headed into the heart of the South Wedge where Irene had lived. The big mysteries had distracted me from my case. I should have listened to Sherlock. Professor Kahlo and the Mayoral office loomed over this detective working on a murder case.

Squalls ripped across the landscape. Without the distraction of car noises and manufactured whines, the sound of the wind overpowered high-pitched spirit screeches, which echoed like all the lost souls of the city pleading for peace. I ducked into a shop entryway and covered my ears, tolerating the chill in deference to needing the silence. Plummeting to a crouch, I shook on my haunches. My left nostril ran. Not for the first time I worried it hinted at a dreadful disease.

Then tears drifted south from my left eye, and I recognized my crisis of faith. I never worried whether God sat in heaven, watching over me. I carried a secular faith in tomorrow, maybe the threat of tomorrow rather than its promise, but still, you need to have conviction about something.

I watched a chipmunk scramble into the center of the road and pause, scanning. When he saw me, his nose twitched at the gust, sniffing for any sign of my intentions. I tried to smell friendly, but I doubt I gave a whiff of anything more than too many nights in the police barracks. With my scent hanging in the air, the small creature turned its tail and ran.

I wiped my cheek with my sleeve and stared at the snot soaking into the fabric. All my clothes bore similar emotional scars. I wondered if people noticed anymore or if we had all settled into an acceptance of carelessness. Across the street, the remains of a clothes shop shifted in the breeze which entered through an open door and a broken window. No one had looted the mannequins. I imagined they would cast a disturbing shadow within the old homestead. I stretched upwards to my full height. As my mind settled, I stepped back into the street.

I stopped at the Partridge place. Shirley sat on the porch, silently watching my approach. "You look awfully grim, like a very serious lawman," she said when I neared within earshot. "I have the impression you might not be bringing good tidings."

"Good tidings don't really fit with the job." I had no idea how to pry loose the information I wanted.

"I suppose it's like taking off a bandage- make it quick and be done with it," said Shirley.

I felt very alone standing at the foot of her porch. What was I thinking not calling for back up from HQ? I wanted to keep matters quiet if possible. The implications for this family and the entire Wedge promised to be too dire when the Mayor became vindictive. "The coffee you turned over to the city, it had problems. Do you know anything you'd care to share?"

Shirley stared away from me into the distance. "Tracy is afraid of things. You can't imagine what the last few years have done to a child.

She gets scared. Lately, she doesn't go near animals. We see a squirrel in the yard, and she screams. We had been here a week when the cats showed up. I don't know where the rat poison came from. I don't know why they put it in the coffee. Danny and David wanted to help."

"I see." I meant it.

"I asked Irene why she had so many cats, but she never said. She never shared, not the type. And another thing, Danny, especially, never really learned you don't cross certain lines. How could he know? What lines haven't we all crossed? Where are the lines anymore?"

"Shirley, this is what I'm trying to do, put a few lines back in place."

"But you can't do this to him. He's a dumb kid," defended Shirley.

"He made sure the bad coffee went downtown. People died in the Mayor's office. Repercussions are inevitable." I knew exactly how this would play out. The slightest hint Danny had caused the mess at the Mayor's place and Shirley would be lucky if they killed Danny quickly and no one else in the family became a victim of city justice. We forgot to strive for modern justice in our infatuation with medieval punishment. Maybe it made it easier when you could not imagine anything fair.

Shirley climbed out of her chair. "What gives you the right? Who says you can be the judge of my boy?"

"I'm not the judge or jury."

"You sure are. You know as well as I do that soon as you voice your suspicions, and you have nothing else, then he's as good as done. No one is going to take the time to think. It only takes a few words." Shirley was right, but nothing she said made Danny innocent. No survivor could claim to be.

"You could send him away?" I suggested.

"No different from a death sentence. He's always had this family looking out for him. He'd never make it on his own, not outside the fences."

"What would you have me do?" I knew the answer and she knew she had me on the ropes. "Look, I have to know what really went down, all of it. What do you know about Irene and her stupid cat?"

"You're damn right about her cats. She started it all." She glanced inside the house through a window. "I'll tell you what I know, and you'll keep us out of it?"

I considered my situation. I did not want an angry fake family of faux musicians chasing me out of the Wedge with murder on their minds. The eyes of Shirley Partridge turned down with the weight of the world. I did not know how to proceed; that would be too much to claim for a single moment in time. Nevertheless, an apocalypse, no matter what the scale, will teach you it is the moments of clarity on which our lives turn- even what our lives seek. Laid out before me, I saw a path leading to the end of my days, a road I could tolerate walking.

"Look," I said, "I want to put things a little closer to fine. Maybe you're correct. I don't know how I'll fix this but let me try to make things as right as they can be. Moreover, if you ask me what putting things right even means, I can't tell you. I can't even promise you'll agree with me, but I can work hard to avoid making things worse."

She surrendered to an inevitable future where she had to trust someone or else run all over again. Something broke loose inside her and she sagged, "Danny's inside."

I found him in the kitchen, playing the ukulele of all things. It sounded terrible. After all he had seen, he had no problem spilling the truth of his misadventures. Irene had been a little weird. Strangers crept around her place. Between them and the black cat, the youngest

Partridges spent too many nights up late with flashbacks to frightening times.

Danny, David, and Shirley took turns talking to Irene, but she refused to discuss changes with them. She denied the strangers even existed, though every Partridge had seen the shadows in the backyard. The cat must have gone into heat and attracted whatever feral felines still wandered the Wedge.

Danny put out a home-brewed concoction of medicine he found in their bathroom cabinet and under the kitchen sink. He ensured the squirrels in the neighborhood would not develop hardened arteries, but his prescription had no effect on the cat population. Next, he hiked to shopping plazas nearby and turned up rat poison. Once again, squirrels expressed interest and ended up buried in the backyard, but the cats ignored the poison completely.

Then, one night, David followed a shadow from their yard to Irene's. The shadow turned into a uniformed soldier when he stepped into the moonlight on Irene's back porch. None of the Partridges could make sense of it, so Shirley went ahead and asked Irene. Irene gave her an earful for her trouble and tossed in a half dozen threats. Danny developed a plan. He paid Irene a visit with a nice cup of coffee. Wary, but appreciative, Irene drank. Next, Danny told her about the stash in the old coffee shop on the corner. He had already dosed the top bags with the last of his rat poison.

I do not have a good reason for what I did next. Mostly I did not want to see another boy die. I felt plenty angry with him, but I had spent the previous year not committing murder. I had been involved in enough of it before then. I knew for a certainty arresting Danny and dragging him before the Mayor only ended one way. Aware everything I did from now on made me judge and jury, I did not want to be his executioner.

I gave Danny my hardest look. "I want to drag your murdering ass downtown and let them do with you what they will, which hurts a great deal and ends worse. You killed someone, many someones, and you can never make any of it right." I leaned in and grabbed him by the shoulder. "But you can try, every single day for the rest of your life."

Then he cried; not what I expected.

***

"I listen to you, and I am not happy," Sarge did not appear particularly unhappy. He leaned back in his chair and a crooked smile wrinkled his cheeks.

Trapped in his office, I felt like a tiny mouse in the den of a sly cat. "I wish I could do something, Sarge."

"I bet you do." His feet hit the floor like paperweights falling off his desk. "I have way too many dead people on my hands to do nothing. People in this city feel skittish. They need answers. The Mayor needs answers. I need a scapegoat." His smile straightened and thinned. His eyes never left me.

"Well, Irene is still..."

"Who gives two shits about her?" said Sarge.

I raised my eyebrow, "The city? The Mayor?"

"Are you really so dumb? I've let you run around on this case as an indulgence because I like you, but feelings change." He let those words rattle around in the room. "This department does not need a detective who won't keep his head up and his eyes open. I can't be everywhere, and I need you to be my eyes and ears in places I can't be."

"What do you want me to say, Sarge?"

"The goddamn Mayor's home," he growled. "What happened there, do you suppose? You went in before our lunatic with the flamethrower turned everything to ashes. Did you see anything? Did somebody go crazy?"

I chewed on Sarge's scenario. The next words out of my mouth could decide Danny's fate and mine. "A definite possibility." And with that, I let the Partridges continue their strange lives.

Sarge studied me carefully. "One of the dead in the break room served as liaison with the Techies. He may have been in contact with the Feds down in Jersey. Didn't you say your scientist had also been in contact with them?"

"I might have." I remembered Sarge had led the raid on the Broadsheet office, so he learned a thing or two from the editor. "What are you thinking?"

"I believe your mad scientist may have crossed a line," said Sarge, "and we see free-range zombies in the city again. I think I don't like him, and I wonder what you could imagine if you'd rub two brain cells together."

"I don't see the connection between Dr. Kahlo and the incident at the Mayor's. There's no motive and I can't see how he committed any crime since he refuses to go outside."

Sarge leaned across his desk. "All right, I'll admit it sounds a little fuzzy, but we already know this Kahlo collaborated with Irene and she went zed. We also know he has political leanings because he's mixed up with the crazy wannabe newspaper."

"I don't really think he's..."

Sarge held up his hand to stop me. "Listen- and now we both know the Mayor is upset about the ordeal his staff has suffered. In addition, you can imagine the sort of conversations he and I have had lately. The

Mayor wants his scapegoat so he can make everyone feel safe again plus look like he is in charge."

He let me mull. I shook my head to adjust to the buzzing.

"Do I have to look around and see what I can see?" said Sarge. "Do I have to tell you this Kahlo guy sounds like a piece of work? According to the Mayor, scientists put us in this mess in the first place."

I made a mental note to downplay my experience as a scientist in the future.

"Who am I to argue with this kind of logic?" Sarge had stopped grinning.

"But he had nothing to do with it." I lost the argument.

"We don't know."

We both should know. "I don't want to be involved in this."

Sarge's voice went soft. "Then you probably should have let yourself be eaten sometime during the last few years, because this life is not for bystanders."

"What do you intend to do?" I asked.

"Nothing, I intend to have you do the heavy lifting. We grab him for questioning on the Irene thing or charge him for keeping a zombie. It's illegal, isn't it? If it isn't then it ought to be. Whatever you decide, you bring him into the station."

I looked hard into Sarge's eyes, hoping for compassion because I needed to believe Kahlo would receive a fair trial. Maybe then I could sleep at night. I saw only broken blood vessels and depths of sadness. "The feds own the professor. The Mayor is not big enough to take them on. I don't know if this is something we want mixed up in, Sarge."

Pity poured off him. "Of course, we don't want to, son, but this became our mess the first time a dead motherfucker sat up and took a bite out of someone. A long time ago the world stopped being about whether or not we want to mix up in it." Sarge waved his hand. "You let me worry about the Mayor."

***

Back in the Wedge, I stood on the college campus outside the professor's building, wondering how I ought to arrest the professor. If the professor made it to the lockup down at the station before the feds noticed, then all to the good. But they might send the cavalry while I hauled him to jail.

I had no backup because I did not want to broadcast my intentions in case the Feds had ears on the force. Someone powerful wanted Professor Kahlo to work on his research. They would not take kindly to his research ending.

As I approached the door, I recognized a figure in the shadows.

"I wondered when you would appear," said Frida.

"Why do you keep lying to me?"

She pouted. "Did I hurt your feelings? I'd hate to think I hurt your feelings. After all you've been through, I'd hate to think I was the straw who broke your back."

I barged past her and banged into a locked door.

"Here, let me," said Frida and she produced a key. Then she blocked the doorway. "So, what are your intentions... here... today...? Regarding the good professor?"

"I am here to arrest him for disturbing the peace by maintaining a pet zombie."

"I can't say this law rings a bell," said Frida.

"You probably need the new code because a lot changed recently."

Frida's expression went grim. "You know this is a death sentence."

"Hell yes, I know it. I thought about dropping the entire thing, but it would mean leaving the city and I'm not emotionally equipped to go, so I'm here and I intend to do my job."

"This is stupid," said Frida. "He's our only hope for finding a cure."

"What a load of crap. I don't know if he's worth more than a bucket of spit, but even if he is, then someone else will have to step up. The good professor managed to be in the wrong place at the wrong time."

Frida said, "A lot of important people will be pissed about this."

"You ever hear the saying about all politics being local. I'd rather not piss off the local powers that be. I'll worry about everybody outside the fences another time."

Frida changed tactics, "The first thing dictators do is kill the smart ones and the free thinkers."

"I don't know which part of your statement is the best: the fact you kept those two groups apart or the bit where you think things are so much worse under the Mayor than under a pile of zeds."

"What about the part where you think I'm talking locally? If nothing else, you must see all this shit created a massive power vacuum which good and bad people are filling, not merely here but everywhere. If you aren't afraid of the Mayor, then you should be. If you don't recognize him as the tip of an excessively big iceberg, then you need to open your eyes." Right in every way which mattered, Frida's words didn't make any difference.

"A wise man told me to focus on the case because everything else leads to madness," I said. "I can't fix the world but maybe I can fix this."

"You're a real son of a bitch, you know?" Frida explained.

"I figured myself out years ago. Now let me see the Professor."

She chewed her words into silence and swallowed them. Then she slammed the door open and entered. I was not worried about stealth. Kahlo seemed unlikely to be a flight risk.

He sat at his table eating more Hostess pastries. Kahlo blinked a little too much when I placed him under arrest, but otherwise maintained a blank expression. He climbed off his high stool and hung his lab coat on the rack in the corner. "Will I need a jacket?" he asked with his first words. Frida shook her head. I apologized, though I don't know why. He shrugged, as good a reaction as any. I led the two of them to the exit.

While Frida locked up behind us, the Professor pushed past me and walked into the sunlight. I understood the urge. "How long has it been?" I asked.

He took a long time to answer. Everything attracted his attention. He studied the sky. He scanned the horizon. Kahlo nudged the ground with his shoes. "I honestly don't know, definitely years. It could be a decade. I wouldn't know." He inhaled deeply, dramatically. "It tastes different."

"It's bound to have been a little stuffy indoors."

Kahlo shook me off. "I mean from before, from the last time. Cleaner- less pollution flavor." He stuck out his tongue and tasted the breeze. "Are people living longer?"

"I wouldn't say so." I gave him a gentle shove. "Most folks say the air smells of death. Of course, considering your companions of late, this may be an improvement."

Kahlo turned to Frida, "I almost forgot about Donald. Will you feed him and watch over him?" No recognition passed between them beyond former student and long-ago professor, even when she nodded her assent.

Frida trailed along behind us by ten paces. We stopped every few blocks as the Prof wanted to take in everything. On a death march, Frida and I dragged our feet. As for the intended victim, he enjoyed a grand outing. If not for his slow stride, we would have lost him every time a new building appeared on the horizon. I felt only relief when the bridge to downtown came into view.

Phil watched our approach. Another slow day guarding the passage, I supposed. In the fading daylight, I caught a grin on his face, but he did not direct it at me. Our Phil took a shine for the unknown Frida. They must have met on her traverses over the zombie pens.

The stench hung lightly, which might have explained the Professor's surprise at the sight spread out below the bridge. Also, he had acclimated to the smell of rotting flesh. I had not observed a first-time visitor to the pens in a long time. The Professor slowly crossed to the edge and looked down. Most people stayed to the center of the road and hurried across. His eyes almost twinkled as though he looked out on a sea of potential experimental subjects.

I shuddered for him, before walking over beside him. "Makes you think?"

"So many lost, why do they keep them?"

"Memories," I muttered. "Every single one down there is a blurry photograph of someone who mattered. The person they mattered to couldn't say goodbye. We kept them in the basement, the attic, the spare bedroom, or the shed or God knows where. It only led to more zombies because people are ridiculous, and they wanted one last hug or something else stupid."

"Blurry photographs..." The professor whispered, "So many children."

"It reminds you how hard it can be to put a bullet in your kid's head." I turned away from the view. "All of us walking around are the ones who found a way to do it. We've built a lovely society, don't you think?"

"I don't know," Kahlo sighed. "Perhaps it's a great attempt to hold on to our humanity in the face of unmanageable insanity." He sounded like a college professor for the first time that day. Then he turned away and stared at the city buildings.

I watched Phil and Frida by the downtown gate, deep in conversation. I had no idea what she had said to him, but tears dripped down Phil's face. She had her hand on his knee. Their heads touched temple to temple. Phil nodded vigorously. Frida wrapped him in her arms. The professor walked away, and I left behind the strange pair in their mournful tableau.

At the station, I directed Kahlo to the stairs behind the front desks. I half expected a hearty greeting, official congratulations, and a pack of junior officers running up to take the vile felon off my hands. When nothing of the sort happened, I prodded the old man forward. His enthusiasm for the journey waned as soon as we re-entered indoors. I too felt the loss as the rest of the process became anticlimactic.

In the big room where everyone kept a desk, nary an eye turned in our direction. It took an introduction to Sarge to gain any traction and then I lost the Professor for good. Two new young bucks whisked him upstairs to the cells and I had finished with the world. Except I had paperwork to complete. No one ever read the forms. I did my own filing and no other steps occurred between my typewriter and the cabinet. We bow in the direction of bureaucracy, like an ancestor we venerate for obscure reasons.

Sarge had gone upstairs with the bucks and Prof. Kahlo. I waited, but he never returned, so I headed to the cafeteria. I landed at a table by the window staring at Sherlock again. "You like the off-hours, don't you?" I asked.

"I'm not the only one," he retorted. Chewing slowly, Sherlock examined me. "You look tired, confused, and sad. I'd draw conclusions, but it is fairly common these days."

"You're not earning your moniker."

He leaned back in his chair. "All right." Sherlock placed his chin on his fist. "You have been out walking. I would say in the South Wedge. You have done something you are not certain is right. I see by your fingertips you have been filling out arrest forms on the typewriter. So, I conclude you have kept your narrow focus and arrested a suspect in the murder case."

I waved my utensils in the air in salute. "You ran into Sarge in the stairwell."

"Detective work," Sherlock smiled, "though not so special when you know how the trick is done."

I let time pass for mutual rumination. "Made any progress on your case? The big picture one?"

"You don't want to hear about it. Seriously, you really don't. It would make God weep."

"I think He's about cried out by now," I said.

"The acts of man and nature will ensure it never happens. In my case, we are talking about men, but, as I said, you don't want to worry your little youthful head. Our Alonzo has done a wonderful job keeping his focus. You have a great future if you can keep it up." He pushed away from the table and walked off.

I stared at his back and thought dark thoughts.

***

Word came from the Mayor's office in the morning. I saw the official notice tacked up on the bulletin board. We would execute Professor Kahlo in two days. His high crime given a name: unregistered zombies. I didn't know we allowed people to harbor registered zombies, but every law had an exception when we needed one; even better if enforcement could be open to the interpretation of the officers involved. I could not scoff at such leeway.

Sarge could not care less what happened to the Professor. He had his hauling team down at the university looting everything they could carry. They had doubtless left Donald a pile of ashes in the courtyard. No one would bother herding him to the pits.

I headed upstairs. We had moved the holding tank to the top floor since all the old cells became uninhabitable or unlockable. We threw people in old offices and locked the door.

Lurch oversaw things, so I tracked him down at a desk in the middle of the level. He told me things had been quiet. A couple of drunks slept it off. Lurch had considered tossing a wife beater out a window. Happily, Kahlo had stayed placid, even after hearing news of his fate. No one had been by to visit other than the officers who had briefly visited to lay eyes on the college professor with the pet zed. I looked in through a small opening in the door and saw Kahlo seated by the window, enjoying the daylight. He had his back to me. He could have been napping.

In an attempt at professional suicide, I decided to protest the death sentence. I had been living day to day for an exceptionally long time. The professor's research suggested the possibility of a return to normalcy. Whether on the right track or not, the professor believed humanity could go back to where it had been in my lifetime. I had not known how seductive such a dream could be until I had tasted it. Real or not, I could not stand by while one nasty execution destroyed my hope. I had one avenue for appeal.

They let me into the Mayor's building with a light frisk, after I dumped anything sharp or dangerous in a bucket. Nobody gave me a number for my bucket, but the biggest goon at the door promised to remember my face. I weaved my way through desks. Everything had returned to its place since the zombie beat down only a few days prior. I found no scorch marks when I glanced down the halls.

I saw Sharon in a red blouse seated behind her desk, sorting folders with the seriousness one would associate with running a large city. No one impeded me as I approached. For the first time, I noticed a name-plate, bearing only the title "Deputy Mayor," It appeared convenient not to have a name appended to it. At least I thought so until I noticed the jagged edge at the end of the second word, as if a predecessor had broken off one end and not sanded the rough seam.

Then I wondered about sandpaper because I had not seen any in a long time.

I had time to consider all this as Sharon did not turn in my direction. Although she focused like a bureaucrat, this also said something about my lack of charisma.

"Honest to God, officer, you have patience which would exhaust an angel," muttered the Deputy Mayor. "Couldn't you at least cough into your hand or something?"

"I tried out politeness to see if it fit."

"And...?" asked Sharon.

"The jury's out, but it doesn't look good."

Sharon's lips curled upwards slightly. "What can I do for you, seeing how I need you to stop looming over me?"

"Maybe I should take this up with the Mayor, but I thought I'd try you first. You know about the Kahlo case. I want to see what we can do for the guy. He's been working with the Feds and international scientists..." I had not thought out my whole rationale.

Sharon slowly shook her head. "He's committed a capital offense. The people want their pound of flesh."

"Which people?" Forget my argument, I thought. I hated public servants who weighed in with the nameless populace. "The people have had enough of death. You think this will help maintain order. Preserving order is not a thing right now. At least this isn't how it's done."

The creases on her face grew deeper. "He committed a capital offense." The Deputy Mayor enunciated carefully.

I knew a dead end when I drove down one. "Can I see the Mayor?"

"You have a death wish? Do you want to lose your job? I am only thinking of you when I say it would be an awfully bad idea."

I leaned across her desk, looming as heavily as possible. "I don't like you very much."

"Let me know when the scale fully tips for you," Sharon closed her folders. "Until then, we don't have anything more to discuss."

I wanted to be petty and knock a glass off her desk. She doomed the professor, but I had the ball rolling. I considered turning on Danny Partridge, but it wouldn't change a single thing for Kahlo. I threw my hands into the air and marched out of the building in a cloud of righteous indignation.

Maybe I didn't know right from wrong, but I knew with absolute clarity I could not let Kahlo's life hang in the balance. You don't watch a father walk into the arms of his carnivorous child without stopping him. It's a this or that decision in the moment, but later the father jumps off the Student Union. Outside the Mayor's house, I stood in the middle of the street rooted to the ground by the failure of morality.

If I surrendered to subjectivity, then what right did I have to be a police officer? How could I recognize anything as right?

Finally, I faced the question which uprooted me. How could anyone find their way?

If I needed to rely on someone's judgment, then why not choose my own? I could not see the Mayor, Sarge, Sharon, or anyone having a greater right to decide the fate of individuals or nations. Professor Kahlo might be a deeply flawed individual, but not evil.

Danny flashed across my brain, and I knew I had made the right decision in his case. I could not turn him in now. They would add him to the execution list and not pardon the professor. I imagined a scenario where I intervened with the executioner. I might be the hero of my own life, but I did not feel born to the role.

Then, a boy came out of the Mayor's office and handed me a leaflet off a pile in his other hand.

Executions had not been a common event in the brief history of reborn Rochester. Criminals who merited the death penalty did not live long enough to reach trial, let alone public execution. Police, zombies, and a fully armed populace took you out if you violated any of the social codes currently in place.

I embodied the early interest the city took in slowing this pattern, but we had not yet formalized public executions. Whatever depraved levels to which we had descended in the past, our people did not support building gallows.

Until today... The Mayor wanted an adequate spectacle.

They invited everyone to the areas of the city overlooking the pits because they planned to send the professor in among the zombies. I could believe it would attract a crowd, and I also understood the appropriateness of the method for a man accused of keeping the undead.

I creased the paper into quarters and watched the boy run off, pausing to hand more leaflets to whomever he passed. He would reach more eyes in the next hour than ever stopped to read the broadsheets. I wondered how many people it would take to stop an execution.

I walked across town to the Broadsheet offices. Their old news hung in tatters from building walls, not inspiring confidence in their medium. I paused in multiple doorways, thinking someone followed me, but I was wrong. I had grown paranoid pondering the Mayor and Sarge. I included Sarge since I could not remain oblivious enough to think he had my interests at heart.

I picked up my pace and arrived at the printer's in no time at all. The door had been broken and badly repaired. I shoved it with two fingers, and it swung awkwardly inward with a loud squeal. Flattened bells lay in a pile on the floor. After a few minutes, a familiar door guard hobbled into the hallway. I did not want another scrape with him. He looked like he felt the same, though he did tap himself in the crotch to reveal he wore a protective cup. Then he raised his fists.

I shrugged. "Can I see the editor?"

He gave it consideration and then lowered his fists. With a responsive shrug, he made room for me to pass. I had to navigate around the remains of furniture on the floor, as well as hold my breath. My former foe smelled ripe.

The door into the newssheet office swung precariously open. The editor sat in his accustomed place. Remarkably, the room looked unchanged. It had not been much to look at previously. The editor appeared a little sadder. The sight of me did nothing for his disposition. I went and perched on his desk. "Have you seen Frida lately?"

He rested his chin on his hand, bemused. "Is this a social or a professional call?"

"Professional."

"Well, then, no," said Ben Franklin.

"Does the answer change if it's a social call?"

"Nope."

I sighed. "If you've seen her in the last couple days, then you know about the execution."

"Sure, the Professor who you sent up."

My current bio preceded me. I really wanted to change my reputation. "I hoped to work something out with you. I'd really like to put a stop to this."

"Found yourself on a runaway train and you want off? Welcome to this life," said Ben.

"I think we can stop this one. What if we find enough people to show up to demand freedom for the Professor?"

"Why in the world would they?" Ben pointed at a nearby leaflet, a match for the one I had received. The delivery boys ran fast.

"Because... I don't know. Isn't it your job to figure out how to incite crowds?"

"Because we've been so good at it so far? If I knew how to locate the people to rise up for their own best interest, do you think the Mayor would still be in power? Do you think the Mayor would let us still be in business?"

I looked at the ceiling. "Frida started this. I know she doesn't want it to go forward..."

"Hold it right there. She didn't arrest the man. I'm looking at the person responsible and you need to own up right now to your responsibility."

"I know I arrested him, but she led me around like a dog on a leash. I never would have met the man without her, and she had to suspect how it would turn out. She'd have to be an idiot not to know the pet zombie of his would be a genuine problem."

"You hid a pretty serious accusation under all your self-denial," said Ben.

"I know. I'm not proud of any aspect of this."

We considered the paucity of items on his desk, deciding if we had any conversation left in us. Ben decided we did. "I'm no fan of the Mayor or those damned bullies he calls a police force, but I might be willing to help you. You might be different from the rest. I doubt it, but I'm willing to take a chance." He fiddled with paper clips. "We'd need to print and distribute something brilliant in the next few hours. It won't be easy, and it won't accomplish what you want it to. You might consider working out a Plan B."

"I'm open to suggestions."

"Have you considered breaking the professor out? It used to work in movies."

"I've considered it." I had thought about a jailbreak, but it would mean freeing him from police headquarters through stealth or violence. Violence would only end in more deaths than his and not change Kahlo's fate. Stealth might work if the professor would cooperate. I was not the person to convince him. Besides, what would I do once I had him out of there? I could not be the man to lead anyone into the great wide-open spaces. I could not find the courage within myself to set foot outside the fences. "It only ends badly."

"You're hoping this is going to play out like Pilate and Barabbas, then?" said Ben. "The Mayor will stand on high and look out at his people, wondering aloud if they would like him to pardon this evil man? And the people will call out with one voice to pardon him?"

"When you say it like that, it sounds like a bad plan."

Ben rose and escorted me to the exit. "I admire you for caring, but you need to see what alternatives you have. I'll put the broadsheet out, but it won't help. Next time, think ahead."

Walking out, I bit my tongue and pushed thoughts of Danny Partridge out of my head. I hoped I would not regret any of my decisions, but I knew an ambush of regrets waited in my future - zombies following me down a slowly dimming hall.

Eleven

I trudged away from the printer's, uncertain of the next steps. I hoped for a glance of Frida, but uncertain what to say if I caught sight of her. I had been used for spiteful, murky purposes. Frida might be cruel and beyond understanding. If so, I would never comprehend any of this. Every way I studied the situation, she looked like another post-apocalyptic lunatic.

I had built an excuse for never understanding while blessing Frida with a reason for all she had done and no need to explain. I spent time trying to catch raindrops. I considered heading to MLK Park, an ideal destination for moping, but I had only one choice: work.

Back at the station house, no one showed enough interest in me to talk, but co-workers did peer in my direction. As a building full of cops, subtlety did not permeate. I had well placed expectations.

I dug into my files which distracted me for a while, especially with the typewriter jamming as if angry with me. I finally tossed a cup of pencils across the room and headed for the stairs. I wanted air and opted for elevation. Before slamming the roof access open, I whispered a prayer Sherlock had gone somewhere else. To my relief, alone I was.

The view presented a city which appeared unchanged. The buildings crumbled on the inside, but they always looked the same from where I stood. Someday, we might cough up a building inspector, but in the meantime, everything stood tall through a combination of hope and ignorance, the two most gravity-defying forces on earth. Right then, I knew it did not matter if the professor and his compatriots ever found a cause or a cure for the epidemic. Those might be answers, but answers can look like endings.

"What are you, a fucking Rodin sculpture?" Sherlock had arrived during my reverie.

"Fuck you and yours," I explained.

"Too late," he smiled. "I came up here and you looked like a useless idiot attempting to comprehend the world. I am familiar with the look. Be careful. It causes wrinkles and sunburn."

"Yea, I don't want to end up like you," I said.

"You could do worse."

"Than daft and lazy?" I asked.

"Plenty of things worse than those," said Sherlock.

"You feel like helping me with a jailbreak?" I asked.

"Speaking of daft things, this would be on the list," said Sherlock.

"I think we're making a mistake executing the professor."

"Probably, but we won't be the first or the last to overstep and you don't have the power to fix any of it," said Sherlock.

"I'd like to think I might fix some of it."

"Then you're fooling yourself." Sherlock squinted into the sun behind me. "What makes you think saving this one man will make anything better for anyone? It might make everything worse."

"I can see why you spend your time up here, paralyzed." I pushed past him.

"Yea, maybe so," he said as he held still, while I moved beyond hearing.

***

As dusk settled, I concluded I never had a plan. Sitting in the barracks, I remained unconvinced a plan awaited conjuring. The radios started. Reflexively, everyone reached for the power switch at sunset and waited for the broadcast.

I realized I had not scanned for other stations in recent memory. I wondered who else might be out there. We did need additional brains to help us think creatively.

Then the broadcast filled the air. News came first, and the execution led off the reporting. Arrive early for the best view because the authorities scheduled it for sunrise. They did not go into detail about the method, but it would be at the pit. I assumed they would herd him inside the cage once someone ended his life.

I could not mourn anymore. I felt worse about feeling nothing than I did about the death. I felt a small stirring when we buried Irene's family in the backyard, but I usually felt nothing more than tired at the burden of one more task. I certainly could not weep anymore, especially after all the people I had not shed tears over.

The apocalypse made strange bedfellows and those strangers had become friends. Watching strangers die could break your heart until finally your heart crystalized. They say people grow used to anything. All the survivors provided proof. The flip side of the thick skin gave me hope no one would be terribly interested in the execution. They might attend from civic fear, but I doubted the Mayor cared. The slaying was the message.

As I analyzed the world, while listening to an old radio show playing off a compact disc found at the library, my interest in saving the professor waned. Inertia took hold. I made my peace with all of it. I did not feel like a bad person anymore, merely stupid, and lazy.

***

Sarge walked through the barracks pounding on anything handy. Curses echoed through the concrete catacombs, as we had not experienced an early morning call in a while. The spring air made us brittle, and my joints ached until they loosened adequately.

By the time I dressed, I heard one of the kitchen ladies squawking some yards away. They had brought us breakfast in bed or as close as could be. Hot coffee and bread guaranteed. If you pushed to the front of the line or the ladies saved something for you, then you might eat fruit or oatmeal. My morning ablutions dragged on and I did not push when I arrived in the queue, so I ended up with the basics. No one saved anything for the likes of me.

I took my coffee on the sidewalk and watched the sunrise slide down the street. The sun lied. The warmth seeped into my bones and deceived me into expecting a good day.

Men filed out of the barracks, heading for their appointed posts, displaying a scattering of riot gear. I noticed I did not have an assignment. Sarge emerged only feet away and paused. We looked at one other, neither saying a word. He looked sad for a moment, I think. Then he left. As he walked away, I realized he wore riot gear too.

Without anything more definite to do, I jogged to Main Street, looking for the new broadsheet. I found nothing and cursed the editor, his staff, and their children. In the end, I felt most angry with myself because I had accomplished zilch. If I spent more time dwelling on it, I could convince myself the professor deserved his fate, or at least none of it mattered. My head concurred. My gut demanded he live. Bread and coffee had not been enough to quiet my gut.

Maybe I needed bread and circuses.

Desperately bored citizens had taken the admonition to heart to arrive early for an unobstructed view. All of us knew sunrise did not mean sunrise. It meant when everyone got around to it and the audience grew as large as it would.

I followed a young couple down Clinton to the crossing bridge. All smiles, they held hands, looking like the future, full of promise, had already come. I wanted to hail them and to explain how utterly wrong they were.

The sun continued to defy my pessimism.

At the bridge, my fellow officers shoved the barriers aside and people pushed up against the western edge. Sharing a healthy dislike of the cage below, no one pressed dangerously close. A few people straggled in from the South Wedge, but most of the spectators came from downtown.

The police spread out and I did not see any friendly faces. None wore the watch uniform either. Phil did not man the bridge. He had always been uncomfortable around crowds. Considering his unusual relationship with the zombies down below, he did not need to see his fellow citizens' expressions of contempt and worse.

The bridge no longer offered a variety of objects the living could rain down on the undead, but the more determined hooligans had brought stones and trash. The police let them have at it until someone hit their mark. From this distance, even the harder hearts on the force did not want to see the results of a sharp rock to a zed's face. Initially, the crowd cheered throws which knocked a walker around, though enthusiasm waned as more joined in with less accuracy.

I had forgotten about the loudspeakers scattered across downtown until the one on the bridge blared into action with a tremendous throat clearing. "Welcome to this morning's execution. It is my great honor to present the Mayor of our flower city, His Honor!"

"Thank you, thank you. I appreciate everyone coming out on this fine morning..."

I know he droned on, but a young man weaving about and passing out leaflets distracted me. When he approached, I curiously took one, less like leaflets and more like scraps of paper, and read it: "We are better than this. Bring back civilization."

Unimpressed by the Broadsheet crew, I acknowledged the professor's fate had been sealed. I saw the fliers tossed aside, dropped over the side of the bridge. Members of the public cuffed the boy as he passed. Random murmurs of support did not translate into action.

My attention returned to the loudspeaker. "...of course. Even so, we cannot permit the unlicensed maintenance of the undead for any purpose. Please respect our rules or expect to pay the price. In conclusion, let me remind you the pits are here for a reason. Please do not give in to your baser desires. The caged undead deserve our pity in their current state. Please do not arouse them with unnecessary vindictive behavior or bombardment. As always, I am your Mayor. Bring me your concerns and we will work together to make Rochester a place where life reigns supreme. Madame Executioner, initiate."

We all flinched as a bombastic click signaled the end of the broadcast.

Everyone looked due west which meant the Mayor had explained the method of execution while my attention had been elsewhere. I pushed my way through the mass of people. Despite their desire to see, they parted for my uniform. Soon enough, I had a good view. I needed my penance for my role in the whole affair.

A detail of cops escorted the professor down the embankment toward the enclosure. During the night, city employees carved rough steps into the dirt. So close to the zombies after sunset must have made it an unpleasant job. Artificial light created its own shadows, which stirred nightmares.

Professor Kahlo bore a dark sweatshirt over the same clothes he wore when I had arrested him. The hood covered his head, keeping him moving forward like blinders on a horse. His clothes hung loose. A plastic tie held fast his hands at his back.

One of the guards beside him brandished a knife. I assumed they had it handy in case their prisoner hesitated, but I decided they intended to use it to free Kahlo's hands right before the final nudge. Kahlo stumbled as he increased his pace. He led the officers, who looked more like an honor guard than an execution party.

Ideas rose to the forefront of my brain. I searched harder for Phil. My thoughts had to be wrong. I hated the way my mind churned.

In my desperate search of nearby faces, I failed to notice the closest ones. A large envelope pushed its way into my hand. Only when I realized this was not more bumping and shoving, did I see a figure forcing its way through the crowd back toward the city. People let her pass because they gained room nearer the action. I called "Frida!" because I knew no other name to shout. She never turned, and I maintained my post. I foresaw the events about to occur below.

The "Professor" turned his head slightly and I could see how tightly someone had cinched the hood. The officers must be idiots. Perhaps

Frida had bribed them. Possibly, they followed orders. All the implications of the staged execution playing out before me offset whatever relief I felt for the real Professor. Yet my relief stopped my hand. I should have shouted a protest or the truth.

None of the spectators disputed this sentence. Frida had been on the bridge and did nothing to stop the proceedings. Did no one care a completely innocent man would die, not even me?

The officers removed the hood. I yelled out his name. The crowd had been subdued, either because the whole spectacle proved exceptionally unspectacular or because they held no specific feelings about the criminal. "Zombie Lover" chants rose into the air, and a small group sang the chorus to "99 Tears", but my voice carried.

Phil turned in my direction. I swear he heard me and nodded.

On one level, I understood what he chose to do. No one could live so close to death without finding it seductive, which should have been the best argument for disposing of the pits, but we never did. We liked living on the precipice, knowing we could look down on the herd of undead anytime we wanted. In a strange way we felt reassured we occupied this place above them. Or we needed the reminder how alike we and the undead might be.

I do not believe anyone else in the crowd saw someone other than the professor heading to his doom. Kahlo had been an unknown and Phil's face usually wore his rebreather. If they did recognize him, then they felt no desire to raise the alarm. I did nothing. I had seen enough in Phil's face in my one brief glance. He would go through with it either way.

This accomplished my goal, so why would I object?

An eerie calm washed over the crowd as the person in charge raised her arms for quiet. She marched in front of Phil and addressed him directly. Someone must have bribed the executioner. Perhaps she had never seen the prisoner. Did she not know Phil? As she spoke, her voice carried over the sound system. "James Enrique Kahlo, Rochester finds you guilty of the most heinous crime of harboring the undead. The punishment is sequestration in the pits!"

Scattered cheers rose, but also gasps. I cannot imagine what those people expected, but this would never end well for the condemned. The guards led their prisoner to a gate in the fence. Two men held his arms tightly, though he showed no sign of resisting. The others shooed nearby zombies away from the entrance. The executioner stepped behind Phil and freed his hands. Then she opened the gate. Quickly, she thrust Phil inside and slammed the gate shut with a metallic clang. The sound echoed, raising the heads and eyes of the zeds.

Phil looked around desperately and ran. He moved to the area below me. He stopped directly below my perch. When he looked up at me, more gasps erupted in the crowd, and I wondered if people finally recognized him.

I realized then what he wanted. "Keep going!" I shouted. Then I turned and forced my way through the crush to the other side. Not the only one trying to move across the bridge, I surfed the flux. I quickly caught sight of Phil, dodging a couple of biters.

His eyes peered upward again, but I could not help him yet. I scanned the pit desperately. Then I saw them, shouted his name, and pointed. He might have called out his gratitude as he turned to run, but I will never know. A zed bit him in the arm for his trouble. Miraculously, his wife and son stood alone on the dirt beside the pavement. They saw him coming and strangely did not move. Poor Phil, however, had a hundred walking corpses shuffling toward him with more after every step. His gait slowed as he shook out his bitten arm. Still, his family held still, their flaccid expressions betrayed nothing.

Phil suddenly shifted as he became aware of his encroaching danger. By this point, he had only a couple steps on his pursuers. Someone yelled, "Run! Run!" Maybe my voice. Either way, he sprinted, stumbling after only a step, but he recovered. He arrived at his wife and son with less than five seconds to spare. With jaw mouthing unheard words, his boy reached out. Always the father, Phil dramatically wiped snot and tears away. The three of them embraced.

The show ended in less than five minutes. The mother stayed true to her cub and screeched at any other zed who approached. Phil took it stoically, emitting only the slightest groan with the first gash from teeth. His neck hovered closest to the boy's mouth, so hopefully those chomps brought a quick end to consciousness. The clothes rolled off his body and Phil toppled to the ground, seeping blood. From where I stood, his smile looked beatific.

The crowd broke up. I made myself watch until Phil became only scattered bones and rags. His wife and child surrendered the corpse after they had overeaten and vomited. The others made certain nothing remained. Originally, I thought Phil had visions of his family restored in a gothic rendering. Nibbled a little, he might go through a painless transition, and enter an awkward embrace.

I realize now he must have known how absurd such an idea must be. He possessed a horrible loneliness he continued to inflict on himself as penance. Someone only needed to offer a path to redemption. The villain needed a name because Frida named only a lie.

I stood alone on the bridge by the time I turned from the horrors below. No guard visible, I wondered how official Phil had been over the last few weeks. We all assumed he would staff the post forever with no one else necessary. Even the barricade remained askew. No longer a checkpoint, the South Wedge fully integrated into the city with this gesture. It could only happen by accident.

I would never alert any other authorities. Someone in charge would eventually notice Phil's absence, but let it be happenstance. Certainly, the evidence of his demise had disappeared.

As I walked, I found the manila envelope still in my hand. I had crushed it when my fist clenched during the morning's events. It bore no writing on the outside. Sealed tight with tape laid over the clasp, I wanted to tear it open for a way to vent, but I saw it as a gift from Pandora. You need to be incredibly careful with those. My fingers fiddled with a dangling tape edge. I made no earnest effort to open the package. Tossing it away lingered as a close-run option.

The police station came into view, and I headed inside. The grunts behind the front desks acknowledged me. Nods greeted my entrance to my floor. I felt like a celebrity without any benefits. Instead of heading for my desk, I made straight for Sarge's office.

"You were nowhere to be seen this morning," Sarge bellowed.

"Then you didn't look too hard," I retorted from outside his door. "I stood right on Phil's bridge."

Soon as Phil's name left my mouth, Sarge leapt to his feet. He dragged me inside and slammed the door of his office. "Let's forget about old Phil, all right? One hell of a cock-up, but Kahlo is nowhere to be found, so, no harm, no foul. Mission accomplished, as we used to say."

"Really?" I said.

"The show went on. Everyone is happy. You're happy, I'm happy, and the Mayor is happy."

"The Mayor has no idea?"

"The Mayor couldn't find his ass with two hands and a map. It's the people around him who worry me." Sarge eyed me. "And you worry me."

Being a worry to Sarge ended badly, but life always does. "You know me, Sarge. I'm not a worry to anybody. In fact, I'm moving out of the barracks in case I say something in my sleep." People did not move out of the barracks by choice unless they formed a family. It required forms.

"Who's the lucky lady?" asked Sarge.

"There isn't one. I know an available place in the Wedge. As your only detective, I think it'll give me space to think. You don't want me ending up on the roof all the time. Besides, it's not as if we're stopping people from going back and forth anymore. We don't have a guard."

Sarge rolled his eyes.

"Are we good?" I asked.

"How am I going to find you when I need you?"

"I'll have my bike. It's not like I won't show up for work."

Sarge looked ready to move on.

I plunged ahead. "One more thing, we need a crime scene team. Do we have anybody with science background?"

"I thought I had you?" said Sarge. "I mostly hire for muscle. It's not like brains come in handy all that often."

"Times are changing, Sarge."

He waved me on my way. "They always do, son."

I saw no reason to delay my move, so I headed to the barracks and packed my things. I hung a sign to ward off any poachers until I had removed everything. It would take multiple trips spread over time.

TWELVE

I pushed my bike across the bridge into the Wedge without looking over the side. The bridge and the view felt barren and forlorn with Phil gone. The sounds and smells emanating from below warned of the abattoir we could all sink into at any time. With my last few steps across, I wondered how sturdy the structure could be.

The bicycle carried my clothes and my books. I pushed it down the street. Massive potholes engulfed the pavement. Weaving as best I could, I nearly toppled my cargo multiple times. The whole way, I thought of Phil and his way out of the slow deterioration of modern life.

I knew people thought we would return to a natural idyll, but the world looked like a crumbling ruin to me, one we spent every day trying to ignore. I passed houses which still stood, but had shifted on their foundations, displaying hideous cracks at ground level. The few people sitting out had vacant or frightened looks permanently burned into their faces. Many showed physical scars which doubtless mirrored the ones in their psyches.

Why did I continue living when so many had died? How could I justify caring about death? Considering my behavior through this entire episode, did I care about life? I embodied a sorry example of the modern detective.

Then again, I personified what we deserved, maybe even what we needed.

***

When Irene's house came into view, I looked upon it with all the hopes of any new homeowner, but I would not let myself enjoy the feeling. The execution had forced me to step outside myself and observe my life from a different point of view. I had to wonder how foolish I might be to harbor hopes for the future. I had no basis for believing a clean couch existed in my future, let alone a beautiful restoration. "I'm not dead yet," I said to no one as I pushed aside my internal commentator.

I liked my new house.

Rolling the bike onto the porch, I leaned it against a post and unloaded. I headed to the bedroom upstairs, which felt like an early vote of confidence in the safety of the South Wedge. Committing to the idea of staying, I spent the afternoon mixing my books in with the ones already there.

Tired by sunset, I turned in early.

***

I rose after sunrise and moseyed onto the front porch. From the steps, I watched the squirrels and birds play in the trees.

"Mr. Crash?" said Danny Partridge. I had heard him approach. He held out a steaming mug. I eyed it suspiciously. "No, it's all right." He had the same endearing offhand manner of his namesake. "Are you moving in?"

"I'm trying it out," I replied.

"Good," he said, scanning the neighborhood.

"Danny, what do you think of this whole Partridge family business?"

He stayed silent for a long time.

I wondered if he had heard me. I almost repeated the question, but I decided it might not be my business.

"I don't particularly like the music. I don't really like having this weird relationship with an odd old TV show." Danny turned to look me in the eye. "But then again, we're the Partridge family which I accept because I don't have any choice. Nobody chooses their family, do they?"

I raised my cup to him. "No, I don't suppose they do."

A small part of me wanted to be a Partridge at that moment and I suppose I became one in a way. Over the coming days, they helped me find my way around the Wedge. I ended up with nice furniture because of their scouting. David pointed out which neighbors to avoid. They had moved the coffee and I never learned where they stored their stashes, but I did not look either. People might like having a cop nearby, but nobody wanted me up in their business, even in this day and age.

I finished my coffee and handed over the empty mug. "You make a fine cup of joe. I appreciate it."

He smiled as if he did not have a care in the world and took off.

I clambered to my feet. Back inside the house, I moved aside Frida's still unopened manila envelope, looking for my badge.

I had to head downtown if I wanted any food. My job entitled me to supplies from the police stores. The cafeteria ladies would all know I lived off base and they would moderate my servings in the lunch line henceforth. Once ready, I rode my bike to the station. The wind picked up and Phil's bridge looked desolate with trash blowing across it.

I did not bother going to my desk. I collected my allotment and bonus cookies for all my hard work lately. I had not expected a windfall from the lunch ladies. Maybe Sherlock missed out for one day.

Standing in front of the station, it no longer felt like home. From a window on high, Sarge looked down on me like a gothic lord who wished me ill. Perhaps he did not, but he did not smile either. Something about the last days had stripped the facade away from the city for me. I could only see the crumbling parts of the buildings. Rochester became zed city and we few remaining souls existed as its denizens, not dead enough to be zombies, but no longer alive.

I felt tired as I approached home, like I had burned through everything I had. Only fumes kept me standing. I stopped to consider my ajar front door. Frida sat at the desk, skimming an old encyclopedia. She looked at me, "This is cool. It's amazing it survived..."

I carried my things to the pantry, tossing words at her, "Everybody didn't throw things away when the world went digital, which turned out to be a blessing."

"Chalk one up for the pack rats," said Frida.

"And zombies destroyed a lot less than ennui and time."

"The most destructive combination," she smiled. Then Frida pointed at the sealed Manila envelope. "You're ignoring me."

"Whatever it is, it's a path I don't want to go down."

"Stopping by the woods on a snowy evening and all?" asked Frida.

"Hunh?"

"You don't know the Robert Frost poem about choosing between two roads? Your horse knows the way and something, something, something."

"Sure, let's blame the horse," I said.

She held silent for a moment. "You're squatting here?"

I showed her the bag of rice I lugged. "Looks like it."

"I had been thinking about doing the same thing. No one should live by themselves; city policy and all."

I sputtered a little and she sat there and let me run out of steam. To my credit, I did not keep it up for long. To her credit, she let the matter of opening the envelope drop. We agreed she could stay and neither of us set any ground rules, so we left it there.

A little later, over bowls of my rice and her cheese, I asked about the execution. Frida had known Phil as long as anyone and had heard his story. She made the dark calculation he would willingly trade places given a little push. She had done nothing more. Phil came up with the plan and told her where to pick up the professor. Frida finished her tale by offering to take me to the Dr. Kahlo in the morning. Apparently, he liked me, despite everything.

"I know your name isn't Frida Kahlo. I don't know if I can sleep under the same roof as someone whose name I don't know."

Frida stretched as though considering my question. "Carol Kester."

I shook my head. "I wasted time watching late night *TV Land* in college. Newhart was a staple."

"You're claiming your name is really Crash, are you?" said Frida.

"It's what everybody knows hereabouts."

"Everybody hereabouts knows me as Carol Kester. You live near the Partridge family, so don't knock my name."

"Fine, but you don't look like a Carol."

"I think we ought to take the opportunity presented by an apocalypse and redefine our stereotypes, don't you?" said Frida/Carol.

Tough logic with which to argue, "You're definitely not related to the professor, at least."

"I never said otherwise. I'm watching a detective piece together all the clues."

"You don't have to be proud of playing me for a fool." I tried to glower.

"You look like something in the rice is making you sick," said Carol/Frida.

I stopped glowering. Instead, I waved my hand in dismissal and left the room.

***

In the morning, I found Carol in the backyard doing something which might have been Tai Chi. She nodded at me and kept moving. I had no desire to be her audience, so I went to my perch on the front steps. Soon enough, Danny showed up with a fresh cup of coffee. After we went through our wordless ritual of confirming it contained no poison, I accepted it. This time, he sat down next to me.

"Word is out about the woman staying here," Danny suppressed either a snicker or a gag.

"Yep," I said.

"I don't want to offend you, but she gives me the creeps."

I considered my little felon for a moment, "You and me both."

"Is she your girlfriend?" Danny asked.

"Nope."

"Mind if I ask her out?"

This gave me pause. "I thought she gave you the creeps."

Danny looked into the middle distance and shrugged. "I've been having a dry spell."

"You and me both."

After minutes of silence, I finished the coffee. Danny took his cup and went home, but not before turning and saying, "I like our little talks."

I stretched and breathed in the air.

Carol bounded onto the porch. "Are you ready to go?"

***

We headed for the university. Carol insisted no one still sought Professor Kahlo. Any meaningful change of venue would interfere with his supply system. Carol figured we could play our cards right and end up the beneficiaries of the professor's largesse. Once it occurred to me that he remained within the city borders, I felt a tremendous sense of relief.

As it turned out, Kahlo had moved into the campus library. Carol had us stop by his old location and pick up gifts. The police had thoroughly ransacked his stores. Sarge's people had cleared out all the foodstuffs. They had burned the miscellaneous zombie parts in trashcans by the door. Decapitated, Donald's remains mummified in his corner of the laboratory. Carol had migrated part of the lab equipment before the official scavengers arrived. Amazingly, Kahlo's handwritten notes remained so we scooped those up and brought them with us.

Carol led me through the university grounds. With the sun in the sky, I pretended this could be any spring day between sessions. The student body would return after a school break, filling every nook and cranny with their vitality. Every shadow held a promise, but nothing would come of it.

The library doors hung ajar, broken long ago. The interior of the airlock remained in place, though unlocked. Inside, the air smelled vile. I hoped the professor did not account for the odor, but I saw him nowhere at hand. We searched. Shelves filled much of the large building. We walked up the central stairs as we failed to locate him on the first floor. Without lights, the further you went toward the walls, the dimmer the rooms became. Carol heard the music first.

We found Professor Kahlo in a dark room, listening to Gilbert and Sullivan. He had found the music collection and wedged the door open. The barely surmountable stench slowed us.

Standing outside the doorway, I turned to Carol, "So, he plugged in the CD player, but hasn't turned on the lights?"

"His benefactors set him up with a brand-new generator because your colleagues took the old one. The building is huge," said Carol. "Lights and air conditioning are beyond the capabilities of any portable generator. Right now, he can't use the computer, which means he hasn't been doing any work. I don't know how long they will let him go on."

Carol settled into a chair opposite the professor. I breathed through my mouth and entered the room. The professor watched us through heavy lids. Moments passed until he reached over and switched off the music. "What do you want?"

Carol laid our burdens on the table. "We brought your notes."

He did not touch the papers. "I missed music. I had forgotten how much."

"Yea," I agreed.

Then the explanation tumbled out of Professor Kahlo, "He came to me and said it was not yet my time. He said I needed to continue living to try to find a cure. He told me I needed to live, and he could arrange it. I didn't ask him to do it. I felt ready. I thought it was my time."

I looked at Carol and she had the same thought I did. Had we broken him? Did Phil sacrifice himself for no reason?

"This place surprised me when I arrived here," the professor gestured toward the collection. "I never imagined anything like this library would still be intact. There are so many books, magazines, and things scattered about." He definitely had been one of those children who dreamt of spending a night locked in a library.

Kahlo slammed his hands down on the table, raising dust and shocking me into inhaling through my nose. I gagged loudly. Whoever had been kind enough to install the generator had not bothered to clean the air filters in the HVAC system. The air looked thick enough to chew.

"Professor, the men who moved you in here must have given you a fresh computer?"

Kahlo chuckled at me. "Hardly, it looks cobbled together."

"All right then. Let's call it new to you. I don't suppose Carol and I could see it?"

Kahlo looked confused.

"Perhaps you know her as Frida?"

Carol smiled, "Marcia, actually."

"For crying out loud," I muttered.

"A rose by any other name...," said the Professor.

"Trust me, you're right," I told him.

Finally, the old man dragged himself upright and moved out of the room. The air improved away from the cramped darkness. I stopped hating my surroundings quite so much. We followed him to the stairs and up another floor. He creaked as he walked, making strange little noises as each foot bore his weight once more. I had not noticed it before, or he had developed new pains. His shoulders slumped more. The weight of the world had finally shifted to him. We all take our turn.

"I did not want the computer near a window since the sunlight makes the screen glare," said Kahlo. "They put it behind the shelves over here."

The air smelled of gasoline. His caretakers had stored here everything which Kahlo would need . Clearly, his patrons worried about the rest of our city rediscovering him. Why not a guard? Why leave the old man to his own devices?

"Professor, is this the first time you've been this alone? I mean Irene kept you company. Her boyfriend stayed..." I trailed off. "Professor, you didn't kill...?"

"Of course not, I am not insane."

I allowed the thought to hang in the air for a minute. "Okay, but they functioned as your protection more than your lab assistants, didn't they?" I looked at Carol, trying to read her history, but she showed me no back pages. "Were Irene and Donald involved with the Feds?"

The university professor had an opinion, "Is there a difference between a lab assistant and a lab spy?"

I stopped my nascent interrogation and gave the computer the once over. It looked fine, though clearly assembled from rummaged parts. I motioned for Carol to come closer. "Do you see that... and that... and there?" The hardware bore multiple references to the University of Buffalo. "Professor, what do you know about the people who brought this to you?"

Kahlo described how interested in him they had acted. After his unhelpful descriptions of military camouflage uniforms, he complained about their failure to provide enough junk food.

I stopped him there. Carol had perused the bookshelves for a while by then. I considered the danger of leaving the old man to his own devices but decided the federals had already made their call. Before we left, I made Kahlo boot up the computer to demonstrate it worked. Carol stood by the library exit when I caught up to her. "You think he'll be all right?"

Carol shrugged, "As much as any of us."

She picked up her pace when the fresh air hit us. I hurried to keep up, but finally decided not to rush. I wanted to think, rather than feel as though I ran headlong into a future. Carol, Frida, or Marcia might be proceeding to her next adventure in pursuit of elusive truth. I wanted to focus on fixing my city. After Rochester, I could raise my head and look around at the larger world. Maybe I had stumbled upon what Sherlock had been talking about all along.

I veered away from the path home and headed downtown, letting Carol go her own way. She shrank to nothingness as she progressed away down the street. A question burned within me, and I planned to find an answer.

Once I hit downtown, I headed for the police station and found Einstein on the stairs. "Did we receive a delivery yesterday?"

Einstein looked at me blankly.

"Supplies, did the caravan come into town?"

"No delivery," Einstein shook his head, "but the caravan came through and stopped. You didn't miss anything. They headed back East after a pit stop. Usually, they do a circle back through Pittsburgh, or occasionally come back the way they went. I heard they had to do a special run in the area."

"Did you see any of them?" I wanted to know one important thing. The supply caravan offered cover to the people who helped the professor. They had brought his new computer back from Buffalo. Could my brother be involved?

"Yea, sure, the usual bunch," confirmed Einstein. "They all look and smell pretty much the same after a long haul."

"I suppose so," I agreed. "Thanks."

"Sure," he said to my back. Einstein probably followed it with daggers. No doubt next in line for the prized role of police detective. We are all saps for a title.

I chose the old ball field as my next destination. Had any trucks hung around? Every block, I changed my mind over whether I wanted my brother to be involved. He might provide much-needed clarity, but I had no idea if the good guys or the bad guys had drafted Kahlo.

It did not matter in my small corner of the world. Even so, I needed to know about the equipment in the basement of the Dickinson house, about the Professor, about those scientists collaborating on a cure (or a curse), and about a dead woman who might have been a good guy or a bad guy.

From a distance, I saw the trucks had departed long ago. All the same, I scoured the parking lot for any clues. No one had cleaned the area in months. The travelers hauled out what they hauled in, which provided no hints for a budding detective. Not for the first time, I wondered what my brother did on the supply runs. We all compromised with the new world order but compromising with boredom could be much more difficult.

The sun set as I turned for home. The hairs on the back of my neck still tingled a little bit as darkness settled. I doubted I would recover from the fear in this lifetime.

I suspected Carol would be waiting for me to demand we leave the city.

Call it cowardice if it makes you feel brave, but I had long ago made peace with my limitations. The first time I took a calm breath was the tour of the city barriers for new citizens. People felt trapped, as if it kept humanity in as much as it kept the zombies out. I could not disagree more. Every night I slept for longer than two hours straight proved to me the power of our barricade. I did not like the person I had been during the bad years. I may not have become the picture of human perfection, but I had changed for the better.

I paused on Phil's bridge and peered over the edge. The undead continued their endless shuffling, a little more vigorously in the twilight, like tiny cells in a Petri dish. I caught sight of Phil's wife and son. They had no memory and no remorse. This could be a kind of peace. The patterns of the undead are hypnotic, but I tore myself away.

The dark streets did not frighten me as I had expected. Occasional lights in windows and emanating noises of life brought comfort. This felt like an evening on patrol. I might well have been the only cop walking the streets of the Wedge that night. Even so, I turned up in my driveway and went inside.

The lights out and no one home; the manila envelope propped upright on the desk. Carol had scrawled three words on it: "Gone to Buffalo."

I sat in the dark room and contemplated the arrangement. I found comfort in the fact she had told me her destination. I considered it highly unlikely I would ever see her again. Feelings for other people had become a dangerous slope in a world with such limited life expectancy so I tried to sort out a more acceptable emotion. I settled on tired.

I crossed the room and found Irene's hurricane lamp. She had been one for planning. Carol planned, but more like a tornado. I set the lamp down on the desk and picked up the envelope. I weighed it carefully and found it wanting. Once I located a good place for it, unopened, on the bookshelf, I went upstairs to bed.

Also by Koj Books

<u>**Read all the Little Books of Pain:**</u>
#1 Hammer Nail Foot
#2 Thick As A Brick
#3 A Book Of Practical Monsters

<u>**For YA, MG, and Young at Heart readers:**</u>
Comic Book Summer

Up until 2025, Koj Books was a one author press with fluctuating support from its publisher/editor/author. Then we released...

Five Raging Hearts: Splatterpunk for the Soul

Three novellas and two short stories from the hearts of Craig Brownlie,
Roxane Llanque, Mathew L. Reyes, Judith Sonnet,
and Wile E. Young, with an introduction by Bitter Karella

About the Author

Craig Brownlie lived in Rochester when he wrote the book you're currently holding. That's no excuse for the liberties he took with the city and its residents.